新托福100+

iBT
文法

許貴運◎著

從《基礎實力養成》，到《進階文法修練》
用輕鬆的三大學習法，一舉拿下100+ 高分！

① 引用歌曲中的「共鳴／感動句」強化大腦記憶，立即連結文法重點。

② 「富創意＋趣味」的口訣和諧音，激起學習文法的動力。

③ 只給重點精闢解析，輕鬆找出文法脈絡、透徹理解文法核心概念。

iBT 文法

作者序

　　這是一本生動活潑的學習英文書籍，以深入淺出的方式引領讀者理解英文文法的各個面向，其中穿插了三個人物串場，喬許善於找出快速的理解文法方式，艾比總是能在英語歌曲中找到相對應的文法概念，而卡麥倫則提供系統性的學習方式，三人各有所長。書中每個單元都提供兩題測驗題，讓讀者測試一下自己對該單元文法概念的理解，測驗題基本上以科技、醫學、時事、人文等主題的文章為主，相當於實際 iBT 的測驗題。本書雖然是以測驗為目標，但輕鬆的編排及撰寫方式也可以讓讀者愉快地學習比較高層次的英文，不會覺得枯燥乏味，跟著單元中所介紹的歌曲學習更是一大亮點，讀者可自行上 Youtube 聽取各個歌曲，有些歌曲平時聽沒有特別注意到其中所牽涉到的文法概念，經由本書點出後，應該會有更進一步的理解和體會。這樣的編撰方式要歸功於倍斯特編輯的企劃，讓筆者有發揮的機會。

許貴運　敬上

iBT 文法

編者序

　　儘管新托福考試已經刪除文法測驗，但文法仍影響學習者在聽説讀寫的表現。書中刪除冗長的文法解釋，考生能迅速掌握考點，以三個不同的人物呈現以下三種學習方式。

1. Abby 引用歌曲中的「共鳴／感動句」強化大腦記憶，立即連結文法重點：用《天堂眼淚》這首歌理解 in heaven 是介系詞片語作為副詞之用，從腦海中的歌詞連結起副詞片語置句尾。

2. Josh 使用「富創意＋趣味」的口訣和諧音：使用了粉絲們的男孩（即 Fanboys）來記憶對等連接詞。

3. Cameron 運用重點精闢解析：輕鬆找出文法脈絡、透徹理解文法核心概念。

　　三種學習法都包含了「HOW」和「EXTRA BONUS」，能用最簡單、濃縮的敘述理解文法。最後要説明的是「實戰句」，它提供了最基礎的文法演練，能強化閱讀和寫作的表現。最後感謝作者許貴運在撰寫時付出很多心思，才能完成這本書，誠摯向您推薦這本書。

編輯部 敬上

≫ Josh 喬許

　　來自南台灣，是個陽光的大男孩，平常喜歡在海邊游泳跟打籃球，運動與嗜好使得他頭腦透別清晰，總是能想到口訣等方式來幫助自己學習英語。每次跟同學提到自己沒花很多時間唸英文同學都不太相信。自己則相信用對的學習方式能幫助自己事半功倍。

≫ Abby 艾比

　　出生於台中，是個資優生且熱愛音樂跟唱歌，每當老師照著講義講解著文法內容時，腦海總是飄到其他地方或者是聯想到自己常聽到的英語歌曲，每個歌曲的旋律像是記憶吐司般將文法考點內建到大腦中，面對英語考試總是effortless，預計高三就要考 IBT 跟 SAT 考試。

≫ Cameron 卡麥倫

　　是個道地的台北人，平常熱愛閱讀，不介意被稱呼為是個宅男，對每個科目的學習總有自己的見解，懂得有系統式的學習，秉持著不求甚解的態度在學習每件事，懂得每個文法的概念跟原理，相信徹底理解後才能應付任何英語考試。

UNIT 1　副詞的功用

單元概述

何謂副詞？有何功用？

副詞是修飾動詞、形容詞、另一副詞或整個句子的詞彙，表示時間（now/then/today）、地點（here/there/up）、狀態（fast/well/happily）、頻率（always/often/never）、程度（almost/hardly/very）、方式（carefully/slowly/correctly）。作為修飾語，副詞可置於句首、句中或句尾，端看所修飾的是動詞、形容詞、另一副詞或整個句子。

010

免除了閱讀傳統文法講義或參考書籍冗長描述，簡單瞭解文蓋概念後，直接寫 TPO。

・以代名詞為例，從 TPO1-30 中找出有代名詞出題的部分，了解 it, its, they, them 分別指代句子中所指的部分。

（p.s 你不需要會解釋一堆文法概念或閱讀一堆文法概念，只需盡快掌握考試技巧獲取理想成績。）

Unit 1 副詞的功用

1.1 文法修行 Let's Go

Q1 請問你都怎麼記憶副詞？有什麼更快的學習方式嗎？

「HOW」

※ 副詞是有點複雜，但也不是那麼難。舉例來說，只要看字尾 ly 或 ily，就可以猜到是副詞，但也不是百分之百如此，也有一些例外，只要把這些例外記住就 OK 啦！譬如，costly（貴重的）、likely（可能的）、lively（活潑的）等皆為形容詞，不是副詞。有點像中文裡副詞和形容詞間的區別，字尾為「地」的是副詞，字尾為「的」的是形容詞，現在也有人把副詞字尾「地」用「的」來代替，但尚未被普遍接受。

「Extra Bonus」

■ 用字尾 ly 或 ily 來辨別副詞，主要是針對狀態和方式副詞，時間、地點、頻率副詞不太適用，需要個別記憶，但也不是很難，因為這三類副詞經常出現，剛開始不熟，久而久之就會搞熟。

■ He got up early today. 他今天很早起床。

■ early 和 today 都是時間副詞，修飾動詞片語 got up。

011

Part I 基礎著 低篇

Part II 進階文法練篇

用口訣等協助記憶，學習更無往不利。

INSTRUCTIONS

「HOW」

■ 副詞無所不在，歌曲裡就很多。Cat Stevens 的歌曲《父與子》（Father and Son）這麼唱著：It's not time to make a change./Just relax, take it easy./You're still young, that's your fault./There's so much you have to know.（還不到改變的時候/放輕鬆，慢慢來/你還年輕，那是你的錯/你要知道的還很多）。裡面的 still（還、仍舊）就是頻副詞，修飾形容詞 young，表達一種狀態。still young 是還年輕的意思，still 一定要擺在 young 之前，中文也是一樣，不能說成年輕還。

「Extra Bonus」

■ 副詞有單字也有片語，副詞片語大多是用來形容動詞，譬如，I will call you in five minutes.（我會在五分鐘內打電話給你），in five minutes 是修飾動詞 call 的副詞片語。

■ It's not time to make a change.中的不定詞片語 to make a change 並不是副詞片語，而是形容名詞 time 的形容詞片語。

■ He comes here to make a change.（他來這裡是為了做改變）中的不定詞片語 to make a change 才是副詞片語，修飾的是動詞 comes。

012

由歌詞強化本身學習到的英語概念，除了本書收錄的歌曲外，也可以將您聽過的所有歌曲應用在英語學習上，讓學習更有活力。

‧改變學習方式，除了閱讀英語學習書籍外，也邊用 youtube 等平台，聆聽看到的歌曲，會有意想不到的學習效果喔！在考試或日常生活中都能用歌曲的回想，迅速連結到文法內容跟相關用法，打造過目不忘的學習效果。

（p.s 一定要多聽歌曲喔！）

Unit 1 副詞的功用

「HOW」

■ 在記憶副詞時可以和句型做聯想，譬如，never、seldom、hardly、rarely 這類否定副詞最常引導倒裝句的出現，by no means、under no circumstances、on no account、in no way、not until、no longer 等否定副詞片語也有同樣的功能。肯定的副詞或副詞片語也能引導倒裝句的出現，但不常見。所以說，副詞的功能雖然主要在修飾，卻可以變化出許多不同的句型，像是很多人懼怕的倒裝句，只要把副詞和句型連結在一起就可以搞懂了。

「Extra Bonus」

■ 以否定副詞或片語引導的倒裝句：
 ‧She hardly stays up.（她很少熬夜）-- Hardly does she stay up.
 ‧I will by no means agree.（我絕不會同意）-- By no means will I agree.

■ 以肯定副詞或片語引導的倒裝句：
 ‧Steve comes here.（史帝夫來到這裡）-- Here comes Steve.
 ‧Two men walked out of the building.（兩個人走出這棟建築）-- Out of the building walked two men.

Part I
基礎實力養成篇

Part II
進階文法修練篇

013

除了前述兩個人物的學習法，可以多閱讀此類學習法，精闢的解析了解原由，還可以免除鬧出笑話的可能。

‧此學習法可以讓你迅速解惑又能掌握該知道的重點，在口語表達上也有極大幫助。

1-2 考試一點靈

文 法加油站

■ 副詞可以置於句首、句中或句尾，一般來說如果修飾的是形容詞，通常放在形容詞的前面，如果修飾的是動詞，通常放在動詞的後面，但也可以放在前面。

· She is very beautiful.

■ 副詞或副詞片語可以放在單獨放在句首或句尾，用來修飾整個句子，注意放在句首時，後面一定要有逗點，而放在句尾時，前面一定要有逗點。

· Clearly, the car accident was caused by drunk driving.

■ 這類可以修飾句子的副詞有 obviously、clearly、probably、happily、fortunately、naturally、unfortunately、luckily 等。

■ 副詞也可以連結句意，但無法作為連結詞，有點類似修飾整個句子的副詞，但放在句首時在後面加上逗點。這類副詞有 otherwise、furthermore、besides、therefore、thus、hence、nevertheless 等。

· He hasn't called the police. Therefore he has to handle the accident by himself.

實 戰句

❶ The old man walks slowly in the park every morning before dawn to stay healthy; ----he would end up in a wheelchair or hospital bed without being able to enjoy sunshine and fresh air freely.

(A) therefore
(B) so
(C) otherwise
(D) moreover

中譯

這位老者每天日出前都到公園裡慢走保持健康，不然就會坐到輪椅或躺到病床上，無法自由地享受陽光和新鮮空氣。

考題最前端

在解題時除了要瞭解句意外，還要注意文法上的結構。這個句子中間出現一個分號（semi-colon），表示連結了兩個句子，所以答案不會是個連結詞，最有可能的是連結前後句意的副詞。四個答案中有三個是順著前面的意思往後推，只有一個是往相反的方向推。would end up 不是過去式，而是與現在事實相反的假設，所以答案是 otherwise。

答案：(C)

文法加油站包含更多面對考試時，你可能還需要的相關文法概念，均依條列式列出，便於考前翻閱。

考題有時候只是針對一長句來出題，實戰句能有效連結考點跟協助考生應考。對於直接寫 TPO 一整篇閱讀有難度的考生，可以先藉由閱讀各單元的實戰句並精讀每個句子跟文法重點後再開始寫 TPO，可以減低自己在準備考試時學習上自信心的喪失並強化學習成果。

CONTENTS
目次

Part **1** 實力養成篇

Part 2 進階文法修練篇

Part 1
實力養成篇

IBT 總分	60-75	75-90
學習規劃	分數段位於 60-75 左右的考生，仍需加強 PART1 實力養成篇前 10 小節的文法概念，例如認識對**副詞**的認識、**代名詞**指代題在閱讀考試中的掌握等等。	分數段位於 75-90 左右的考生，則需加強 PART1 實力養成篇後 7 小節的文法概念，除了**指示代名詞**用法差異外，仍需掌握**關係代名詞**的用法和應用。
延伸學習	**L** 注意聽力時，名詞的單複數等。	**L** 注意聽力時，關係代名詞修飾先行詞的描述。
	S 口說中避免形容詞和副詞同形者的誤用，並注意指示代名詞的使用。	**S** 可以多使用關係代名詞等長句，讓語句更豐富多變，分數更高。
	R 需注意代名詞指代題中，**it, its, them, they** 所分別指代對象為何。	**R** 多注意插入題時，選項因為句子變長而受到干擾。
	W 必免在誤用形容詞和副詞，以及注意語序跟用字。	**W** 使用關係代名詞強化語句表達。注意語句的主動詞一致性，避免失分。

副詞的功用

單 元概述

何謂副詞？有何功用？

副詞是修飾動詞、形容詞、另一副詞或整個句子的詞彙，表示時間（now/then/today）、地點（here/there/up）、狀態（fast/well/happily）、頻率（always/often/never）、程度（almost/hardly/very）、方式（carefully/slowly/correctly）。作為修飾語，副詞可置於句首、句中或句尾，端看所修飾的是動詞、形容詞、另一副詞或整個句子。

1-1 文法修行 Let's Go

Q1 請問你都怎麼記憶副詞？有什麼更快的學習方式嗎？

「**HOW**」

■ 副詞是有點複雜，但也不是那麼難。舉例來說，只要看到字尾 ly 或 ily，就可以猜到是副詞，但也不是百分之百如此，也有一些例外，只要把這些例外記住就 OK 啦！譬如，costly（貴重的）、likely（可能的）、lively（活潑的）等皆為形容詞，不是副詞。有點像中文裡副詞和形容詞間的區別，字尾為「地」的是副詞，字尾為「的」是形容詞，現在也有人把副詞字尾「地」用「的」來代替，但尚未被普遍接受。

「**Extra Bonus**」

■ 用字尾 ly 或 ily 來辨別副詞，主要是針對狀態和方式副詞，時間、地點、頻率副詞不太適用，需要個別記憶，但也不是很難，因為這三類副詞經常出現，剛開始不熟，久而久之就會搞熟。

■ He got up early today. 他今天很早起床。

■ early 和 today 都是時間副詞，修飾動詞片語 got up。

「HOW」

■ 副詞無所不在，歌曲裡就很多。Cat Stevens 的歌曲《父與子》（Father and Son）這麼唱著：It's not time to make a change,/Just relax, take it easy./You're still young, that's your fault,/There's so much you have to know.（還不到改變的時候/放輕鬆，慢慢來/你還年輕，那是你的錯/你要知道的還很多）。裡面的 still（還，仍舊）就是個副詞，修飾形容詞 young，表達一種狀態。still young 是還年輕的意思，still 一定要擺在 young 之前，中文也是一樣，不能說成年輕還。

「Extra Bonus」

■ 副詞有單字也有片語，副詞片語大多是用來形容動詞，譬如，I will call you in five minutes.（我會在五分鐘內打電話給你），in five minutes 是修飾動詞 call 的副詞片語。

■ It's not time to make a change. 中的不定詞片語 to make a change 並不是副詞片語，而是形容名詞 time 的形容詞片語。

■ He comes here to make a change.（他來這裡是為了做改變）中的不定詞片語 to make a change 才是副詞片語，修飾的是動詞 comes。

「HOW」

■ 在記憶副詞時可以和句型做聯想，譬如，never、seldom, hardly、rarely 這類否定副詞最常引導倒裝句的出現，by no means、under no circumstances、on no account、in no way、not until、no longer 等否定副詞片語也有同樣的功能。肯定的副詞或副詞片語也能引導倒裝句的出現，但不常見。所以說，副詞的功能雖然主要在修飾，卻可以變化出許多不同的句型，像是很多人懼怕的倒裝句，只要把副詞和句型連結在一起就可以搞懂了。

「Extra Bonus」

■ 以否定副詞或片語引導的倒裝句：

· She hardly stays up.（她很少熬夜）-- Hardly does she stay up.

· I will by no means agree.（我絕不會同意）-- By no means will I agree.

■ 以肯定副詞或片語引導的倒裝句：

· Steve comes here.（史帝夫來到這裡）-- Here comes Steve.

· Two men walked out of the building.（兩個人走出這棟建築）-- Out of the building walked two men.

1-2 考試一點靈

文 法加油站

■ 副詞可以置於句首、句中或句尾，一般來說如果修飾的是形容詞，通常放在形容詞的前面，如果修飾的是動詞，通常放在動詞的後面，但也可以放在前面。

- The servant slowly opened the door for the guest./The servant opened the door slowly for the guest.

■ 副詞或副詞片語可以放在單獨放在句首或句尾，用來修飾整個句子，注意放在句首時，後面一定要有逗點，而放在句尾時，前面一定要有逗點。

- Clearly, the car accident was caused by drunk driving.

■ 這類可以修飾句子的副詞有 obviously、clearly、probably、happily、fortunately、naturally、unfortunately、luckily 等。

■ 副詞也可以連結句意，但無法作為連結詞，有點類似修飾整個句子的副詞，但放在句首時在後面加上逗點。這類副詞有 otherwise、furthermore、besides、therefore、thus、hence、nevertheless 等。

- He hasn't called the police. Therefore, he has to handle the accident by himself.

實 戰句

❶ **The old man walks slowly in the park every morning before dawn to stay healthy; -----he would end up in a wheelchair or hospital bed without being able to enjoy sunshine and fresh air freely.**

(A) therefore

(B) so

(C) otherwise

(D) moreover

中譯

　　這位老者每天日出前都到公園裡慢走保持健康，不然就會坐到輪椅或躺到病床上，無法自由地享受陽光和新鮮空氣。

考題最前端

　　在解題時除了要瞭解句意外，還要注意文法上的結構。這個句子中間出現一個分號（semi-colon），表示連結了兩個句子，所以答案不會是個連結詞，最有可能的是連結前後句意的副詞。四個答案中有三個是順著前面的意思往後推，只有一個是往相反的方向推。would end up 不是過去式，而是與現在事實相反的假設，所以答案是 otherwise。

答案：(C)

文 法加油站

■ 副詞中最常見的時間副詞和地方副詞通常有先後順序，地方副詞要擺在時間副詞之前，但時間副詞也可以擺在句首，讓地方副詞留在句尾。

- I saw my friend John in the park last night./Last night, I saw my friend John in the park.
- Students go to school every day.
- I met an old friend at a restaurant in a small village in Changhua County last week.

■ 有好幾個地方副詞時，要按照小地方到大地方的順序排列，in a small village 是小地方，in Changhua County 則是大地方。

■ 除了上面提過的之外，還有一些常見的詞彙也是副詞，如果沒有提醒，可能就會忘了它們原來也是副詞，像是 either、neither、too、yes、no。

- She can run very fast; I can run very fast, too.
- Paul can't swim. Neither can I.
- Did you make the mistake? Yes, I did.

實 戰句

❷ -----do we notice that we lie more often than we are cheated partly because we take some of our lies as harmless and partly because we always feel that we are honest people, not liars.

(A) Often

(B) However

(C) Carefully

(D) Seldom

中譯

我們很少注意到我們說謊的次數多於我們被騙的次數，部分是因為我們認為我們的某些謊話是無害的，部分則是因為我們總是覺得自己是誠實的人，不是說謊者。

考題最前端

這一題是測驗你對倒裝句的熟悉程度，倒裝句通常是由否定副詞引導，四個選項中只有一個是否定副詞。這種刪去法通常是用在你對題意或答案不確定時，如果你對倒裝句很熟，就可以更快地找出答案。because 引導出表示原因的副詞子句，功能在修飾前面的主要子句。

答案：(D)

區分代名詞 it 和 its

單 元概述

it 和 its 作為代名詞有何功用及差別？

代名詞 it 通常指事物和動物，也可指人，主格和受格同形，但所有格則為 its，記得這個口訣：it—it—its（第三人稱單數，複數則為 they—them—their）。It 常常被用作虛主詞，引導後面的不定詞片語或 that 子句，而 its 主要是放在名詞前的所有格形容詞（如 Every dog has its day）。

2-1 文法修行 Let's Go

Q2 請問你都怎麼記憶 it 和 its？有什麼更快的學習方式嗎？

「HOW」

■ it 和 its 相當於中文的「它」和「它的」，但「它」和「它的」在中文裡的使用頻率遠不及英文的 it 和 its，沒得比。說 it 無所不在一點也不為過，但 its 的出現頻率卻少很多，遠遠比不上 it's。

■ it's 是 it is 的縮寫，不是所有格，此 its 非 it's，許多人常常搞錯，這也難怪，中文沒有 it's 這種縮寫。雖說 it 無所不在，但常常只是擔任虛主詞和虛受詞的角色，有點像是個工具人。

「Extra Bonus」

■ 如果提到的是時間、天氣、氣溫、距離、或現在的狀況，要用 it 作為主詞，像是 It is ten o'clock.或 It is ten kilometers to the train station. 中文會說現在十點及離車站有十公里，我們不會說 Now is ten o'clock，還是要用 it 來表示時間。

「HOW」

■ Neil Young（尼爾·楊）有一首叫做《金心》（Heart of Gold）的歌，裡面提到 I want to live,/I want to give/I've been a miner for a heart of gold./It's these expressions/I never give/That keep me searching for a heart of gold.（我想要活/我想要給/我一直是個挖掘金心的礦工/就是這些我/從沒給予的詞語/讓我繼續尋找金心）。

■ It's these expression 中的 It's 是 It is 的縮寫，而不是所有格 its。英文歌曲中通常把 it is 縮寫為 its，很少維持原樣，因為 it is 是兩個字，念起來為兩個音節，而縮寫 its 則是一個字，一個音節。

「Extra Bonus」

■ It's 除了為 it is 的縮寫外，也可代表 it has。It's amazing.和 It's got to be a mistake.這兩個句子，前面是 It is，後面才是 It has.

■ It's these expressions 中的主詞是 it，而 these expressions 為其補語，雖然是複數，但動詞要跟著主詞走。

■ It's these expressions that keep me searching for a heart of gold.中的 expressions 是被 that 引導的形容詞子句修飾的先行詞。

「HOW」

■ 測驗時要先把句子的主詞和動詞找出來，就可以輕易地區分 it's 和 its，例如：It's necessary to read a good book. Its content can be helpful.前面句子裡的 It's necessary 是 It is necessary，為引導後面不定詞 to read a good book 的虛主詞，而後面句子的 its 則是所有格形容詞，若出題者把 its 改成 it's，還是會有人搞錯。句子裡的主詞是 content，can 是助動詞，後面接原形 be 動詞，如果把句子改成 It's content can be helpful.就不通了。平時閱讀時多做一些句型分析會很有幫助。

「Extra Bonus」

■ 如果還是搞不清楚，記得 it's 出現的頻率遠大於 its，這樣考試時就比較不會完全毫無頭緒。

■ It is 和 it has 的縮寫都是 it's，兩者最大的差別在於後面跟的字，如果是補語，那就是 it is，後面跟的如果是動詞的過去分詞，則是 it has。

2-2 考試一點靈

文 法加油站

■ It 作為虛主詞和虛受詞經常和不定詞一起使用,用來引導出真正的主詞和受詞,雖然是虛的,卻是必要的一部分。

- It is important to get up early but many people find it difficult to keep the habit.

■ It 和 seem 及 appear 等動詞形成 it seems that 和 it appears that 句型,碰上這類句型就不用擔心是否要用到 it's,因為它們不是用現在式就是過去式,沒有完成式。

- It seems that the boy enjoys playing baseball.(可以改為 The boy seems to enjoy playing baseball.)

■ It 可以用來代替 nothing、everything 和 all。

- Everything's all right, isn't it?

實 戰句

❶ The universe has a logic of its own, which we often find-
----hard to understand because there are still many
things out there beyond our understanding. All we can
do is to imagine.

(A) its

(B) it's

(C) it

(D) them

中譯

宇宙自有其運行之道，我們通常覺得很難理解，因為外面還有許多超出我們理解範圍的東西。我們能做的就是想像。

考題最前端

這題各有一個 its 和 it，a logic of its own 源自 something of one's own 這個常用片語，英國小說家維吉妮亞‧伍爾夫（Virginia Woolf）寫了一篇叫做《自己的房間》（A Room of One's Own）的作品，名稱就是 something of one's own 這個片語的衍生。句子裡還套用另一句型，即 find it difficult, hard, or interesting to do something，很明顯，空格裡缺的是 it。

答案：(C)

文 法加油站

■ 除了 It seems that 和 It appears that 這兩個常用的句型外，It happens/proves/turns out that 也很重要。

· It happened that I came across an old friend yesterday. （等於 I happened to come across an old friend yesterday.）

■ It is+形容詞+of+人+to 不定詞是一個形容人的某種特質的句型，這類形容詞有 kind、good、nice、polite、rude、brave、smart、wise、foolish、careless 等。

· It is kind of you to let me come.

■ It is said that 這個句型更是常見，等於 They say that 或 People say that。這個句型除了可用 say 外，還能套用 believe、expect、know、think 等動詞來表達類似的意義。

· They say that the teacher is sick. （也可以説 It is said that the teacher is sick.或 The teacher is said to be sick.

實 ▶ **戰句**

❷ **Despite-----extensive use, a climate change measurement like global warming potential does not provide an effective solution to reducing greenhouse gases affecting the environment. There is still much room for improvement.**

(A) it

(B) its

(C) their

(D) the

中譯

　　然而儘管被廣泛地採用，全球暖化潛勢之類的氣候變遷測量標準沒有為如何減少影響環境的溫室氣體提供有效的解決方案。還有很大的改善空間。

考題最前端

　　這一題主要在探討氣候變遷議題。首先，我們先做句型分析。句子的主詞是 a climate change measurement，後面的 like global warming potential 是修飾主詞的形容詞片語，動詞是 provide。句首以 despite 開始的介係詞片語是修飾整個句子的副詞片語，所以空格裡缺的是第三人稱單數代名詞的所有格，也就是代表事物的 its。

答案：(B)

區分代名詞 they 跟 them

單 元概述

They 和 them 之間的差別？

They 和 them 都是代名詞，用來代替複數的名詞，為第三人稱代名詞的複數形式。兩者之間的差別在於 they 是主格代名詞，them 是受格代名詞。They 代表兩個或兩個以上的人或事物，them 也是如此，只不過一個是在主詞的位置，另一個則是在受詞的位置。

3-1 文法修行 Let's Go

Q3 請問你都怎麼記憶 they 和 them？有什麼更快的學習方式嗎？

「HOW」

■ 以中文來說，they 和 them 都是他們，沒有主格和受格之分，那要如何記憶它們呢？說真的，好像沒有甚麼快速記憶法，只能用 I-me，we-us，you-you，he-him，she-her，it-it，they-them 這樣的口訣來加以記憶，這些主格受格的變化，只有第二人稱單複數同形的 you 和第三人稱單數的 it 最有規律，其他的都要強記下來，就像背九九乘法表一樣，反覆地唸，順口之後就會慢慢地記住。

「Extra Bonus」

■ They 和 them 有時可以代替 he 或 she，尤其是指涉不定代名詞時，像是 somebody、anybody、nobody 等。例句：If anybody wants my ticket, they can have it.

「HOW」

- 歐帝斯‧里丁（Otis Reading）所唱的《獨坐在海灣碼頭》（Sittin' on）The Rock of the Bay）有這樣的歌詞：Sittin' in the morning sun/I'll be sittin' when the evening comes/Watching the ships roll in/Then I watch them roll away again.（坐在早晨的陽光裡/我會坐到傍晚來臨/看著船隻駛入/然後又看著它們駛離）。歌詞裡的 them 是 watch 的受詞，指的是 the ships，要先有 the ships 才有 they，they 是代替前面提過的人或事物。如果是 watch a ship，那麼就要用 it 來代替它。

「Extra Bonus」

- They 有時候放到句首是指一般人，不是某些特定的人。例如：They say that it will take several days to get the job done.
- Them 可以作為直接受詞代名詞，也可以作為間接受詞代名詞。例如：Remember to buy some apples. I'll eat them for dinner.（直接受詞）The dogs were really excited. John gave them some food.（間接受詞）
- They 放在句首也可以指特定的一群人，例如：They don't like noise around here.

「**HOW**」

■ 要區別 they 和 them，首先看它們出現的位置，they 會出現在句首，them 則不會（就算倒裝句也不會）。them 通常出現在句中，作為動詞的直接或間接受詞。

■ They 和 them 都有可能出現在句尾，例如：We scored as many goals as they scored. She can sing as well as they sing. 如果把 scored 和 sing 這兩個動詞拿掉，they 換成 them 也通。The teacher is angry with both of them. /Do you know them?/ Don't be angry with them. You are above them. 都是 them 在句尾的例子。Both of them 這個片語需要在介系詞 of 後面擺上受詞 them。

「**Extra Bonus**」

■ It takes somebody+多少時間+to do something 這個句型中的 somebody 是受格形式，例如：It took them an hour to do the job.

■ It is kind of you to let me come. 這個句子改成第三人稱複數就是 It is kind of them to let me come. 介系詞後面只能用受格。

3-2 考試一點靈

文 法加油站

■ 除了 They 和 them 這兩個主格和受格代名詞外，第三人稱複數代名詞還有複數所有格形容詞 their，複數所有格代名詞 theirs，及反身代名詞 themselves。

· They promised to keep the secret to themselves.

■ They 除了指特定一群人，還可以指不特定的人或不限定性別的一群人，最常被用來代替不定代名詞。

· Each and every one of my colleagues will express their opinion about the issue.

■ 介系詞片語是由介系詞加上受詞構成，受詞為名詞時維持原樣（如 in front of the car），若為代名詞則要以受格形式出現（如 in front of them）。

· Don't be afraid of them.

實 戰句

❶ **In an experiment in which spoken sentences were presented to Taiwan's elementary school students, -----, for example, understood the sentence "The man has a**

good wife, and he likes his wife very much," but had difficulties in understanding the sentence "The man who has a good wife likes his wife very much."

(A) them

(B) they

(C) their

(D) themselves

中譯

　　在一個實驗中，台灣小學生聽到一些口說的句子，舉例來說，他們了解「這個人有個好妻子，他非常喜歡他的妻子」這個句子，卻不太理解「這個有位好妻子的男子非常喜歡他的妻子」這個句子。

考題最前端

　　碰到比較複雜的句子時，不要慌張，先找出整個句子的主詞和動詞。句首以介系詞 in 開頭的介係詞片語顯然不可能是主詞，片語中的形容詞子句 in which spoken sentences were presented to Taiwan's elementary school students 容易讓別人以為是主要子句，事實時只是在修飾 experiment，真正的主要子句在後面，空格裡缺的是主詞，動詞是 understood。四個選項中只有 they 可以當主詞。

答案：(B)

■ They 可以和反身代名詞 themselves 一起用，表示強調之意。

　・ They themselves didn't know the answer.

■ Their 和 theirs 也經常被搞錯，前者是所有格形容詞，後面要接名詞，theirs 是所有格代名詞，不用再加名詞。

　・ Bobo is their dog.

　・ The dog is theirs.

■ Theirs 等於 their+名詞，可以放在主詞的位置，也可以作為主詞補語。

　・ Theirs（Their idea）is a better idea.

實 戰句

❷ **When I asked for a product of a particular kind, the clerk told me, "They do not make-----now." She emphasized the "They," which made me feel that I just couldn't find what I wanted.**

(A) they

(B) their

(C) themselves

(D) them

中譯

　　當我問是否有某一類型的產品時，店員告訴我，「他們現在不生產那些了。」她說話時特別強調「他們」，這讓我覺得我就是找不到我想要的東西。

考題最前端

　　這一題是在測驗基本文法概念，既然"They do not make them now." 這個句子有了 they 作為主詞，接下來再出現的只會是受格的 them，如果還是不確定，記得 make 動詞後要接受詞，所以答案就出來了。

答案：(D)

分辨可數與不可數名詞

單 元概述

何謂可數與不可數名詞？

名詞分為可數和不可數名詞，可數名詞前面要加不定冠詞（a/an）、定冠詞（the）、及所有格形容詞（my、your 等），不可數名詞沒有複數，不用在前面加冠詞。可數名詞有普通名詞（table、chair、house、book 等）和集合名詞（family、class、team、people 等），不可數名詞有物質名詞（coffee、tea、sugar、milk、gold 等）、抽象名詞（happiness、love、peace 等）、及專有名詞（New York、London、January 等）。

4-1 文法修行 Let's Go

Q4 請問你都怎麼記憶可數與不可數名詞？有什麼更快的學習方式嗎？

「HOW」

■ 可數與不可數名詞的最大差異在於前面要不要加定冠詞或不定冠詞，而不可數名詞雖然原則上都是單數形式，但有時也可以複數形式出現，讓人有點搞不清楚什麼時候該用複數。

■ 以 coffee 和 tea 為例，平時提到咖啡和茶時，那是一種物質名詞的概念，不是指某一特定的茶飲或咖啡。但如果到咖啡廳或茶店消費時，就要使用 coffee 和 tea 的複數來表示多少杯，像是 three coffees 和 two teas。

「Extra Bonus」

■ Family 是集合名詞，通常是指家庭，如果用到 families，應該是指好幾個家庭，不過現在也可以指家人，像是常見的廣告詞 We are families.

「HOW」

■ 歌手克莉絲汀娜‧佩里（Christina Perri）在《千年》（A Thousand Years）這首歌中唱到：Time stands still/Beauty in all she is/I will be brave/I will not let anything take away/What's standing in front of me（時間靜止不動/她全身上下都美/我會勇敢/我不會讓任何事情拿走/我眼前的一切）。

■ Time 和 beauty 都是不可數名詞，時間和美屬於抽象名詞，無法具象化，同類的名詞還有 friendship、courage、love、anger、hatred 等。Time is money. 這個常見諺語中的 time 和 money 都是不可數名詞，不用加任何冠詞。

「Extra Bonus」

■ 很多不可數名詞也有複數形式，time 代表時間時是完全地不可數，若是代表次數，則為可數。同樣地，beauty 可以表示抽象的美，也可以指某一特定的美人或美事。

「HOW」

■ 不可數名詞也可以量化，但名詞本身沒有變化，只是在前面加了表示形狀、容器、單位的名詞，這一點很重要。牛奶本身不可數，但可以用 a bottle of milk 來表示一瓶牛奶。

■ 正常來講，一杯咖啡應該是 a cup of coffee，但咖啡廳通常就用 two or three coffees 來表示複數杯，簡單方便。另外常見的同類詞語還有 a piece of paper、a slice of bread、a glass of water、a pound of butter、two spoonfuls of sugar 等。

「Extra Bonus」

■ 國名或品牌名稱是專有名詞，一般來說不可數，但有時也可以變成普通名詞。

- An isolated China（被孤立的中國）
- An Audi（一輛奧迪車）

1-2 考試一點靈

文 法加油站

■ 某些物質名詞可以變成普通名詞，但意思和原來的不太一樣。

· Mr. Liu knows a lot of international news from reading an English paper（newspaper）.

■ 抽象名詞也有變成普通名詞的機會，表示具體的行為或事蹟。

· Thank you for your many kindnesses.（表示多次受到熱切的招待）

■ 專有名詞變成普通名詞的例子還不少，通常表示某一特定的狀態。

· Tom was born in Taipei. He had a photo which showed the Taipei 30 years ago.

I
基礎實力養成篇

Part
II
進階文法修練篇

實 戰句

❶ **The first reason for human beings to travel to Mars is the-----of a dream. Sending a manned spaceship to Mars will become an adventure available to an increasing number of people in the future.**

(A) realize

(B) realizing

(C) realization

(D) realized

中譯

　　人類到火星旅行的首要原因是要實現一個夢想。派遣有人太空船上火星未來將成為一個越來越多人享用得到的探險。

考題最前端

　　這一題的主詞是 the first reason，動詞是 is，後面是主詞補語。空格裡缺的是一個可以擺在定冠詞 the 後面的字，很顯然是一個名詞，也就是 realize 的名詞 realization。或許有人選 realizing，以為動名詞也可以，但動名詞的用法是直接接受詞（realizing a dream），不會說成 the realizing of a dream。

答案：(C)

文 法加油站

■ 集合名詞包括 army、crowd、audience family、team、club、class、crew、group、staff、police、people 等，大部分是可數名詞，但 police、people、cattle 本身就是複數形式。

　　・ The police are looking for a thief.

■ 集合名詞可接單數動詞，也可接複數動詞，但單數動詞的機會較多。以 family 為例，若重點在家庭的每個成員，就用複數動詞。

　　・ My family are all baseball fans.

■ 數字通常被當成一個整體，要搭配單數動詞。

　　・ A hundred dollars is not enough to buy a bicycle.

實 戰句

❷ **A recent study found that the majority of people who increased their-----of water by 1 percent reduced their total daily calorie intake. The study examined the dietary habits of more than 18,000 adults in the U.S.**

(A) consumer

(B) consume

(C) consuming

(D) consumption

中譯

　　最近一份研究發現每日增加 1%飲水量的人大多可以減少每日的卡洛里總攝取量,這份研究檢視了超過 1 萬 8000 名美國成年人的飲食習慣。

考題最前端

　　這一題是以 find+that 子句為主的句型,主詞是 study,動詞是 found,而 that 子句裡的主詞是 the majority of people,動詞是 reduced,who increased…percent 是形容 people 的形容詞子句,who 是主格關係代名詞,其動詞是 increased,後面缺的是一個受詞,答案選項裡只有 consumption 符合。

答案:(D)

了解學科名稱

單 元概述

學科名稱有哪些？一定要用單數嗎？

上大學以前，學生讀的學科（subject）比較單純，就是英文（English）、國文（Mandarin）、歷史（History）、地理（Geography）、數學（Mathematics，簡稱 Maths 或 Math）等，這些學科大多是單數形式，只有數學是複數形式，不管是單數還是複數形式，學科都是要接單數動詞。

5-1 文法修行 Let's Go

Q3 請問你都怎麼記憶學科名稱？有什麼更快的學習方式嗎？

「HOW」

■ 其實也沒那麼難，複數形式的學科名稱大多是在字尾加 s，沒有什麼其他不規則的變化，只要稍微留意一下即可。常見的學科有物理學（physics）、數學（mathematics）、統計學（statistics）、經濟學（economics）、（politics）、語言學（linguistics）、美學（aesthetics）、力學（mechanics）等。See! 是不是很有規律，但你要先對它們有印象，沒印象就算碰到也不認識，考試照樣出錯，所以先讓自己認識一下這些學科。

「Extra Bonus」

■ 數學是 Mathematics，和算術（Arithmetic）不太一樣，許多人常常搞錯，算術是數學的一部分，重點在於加減乘除（addition, subtraction, multiplication and division）的運算，數學的範圍更廣。

「HOW」

■ 有一首英語教學歌曲叫做《你最喜歡的科目是什麼？》（What's your favorite subject?），歌詞先重複問 What's your favorite subject? 這個問題四次，然後再唱出四個答案：I like math./I like art./I like science./I like P.E.。接著又問 What's your favorite subject? 四次，這次的回答是：I like music./I like English./I like social science./I like art. 這樣反覆唱出學科名稱可以加深印象，不會忘記。台灣這裡的科目還有國語（Mandarin）、公民（Civics），不妨在練唱時加入，讓英語教學本土化。

「Extra Bonus」

■ 體育課是 physical education，簡稱 P.E.，也可以稱為 exercise course，就是運動課的意思，athletics 則是指範圍更廣的體育運動。還有所謂的通識課程，英文為 General Education，簡稱 G.E.。

「HOW」

■ 以複數形式出現的學科名稱，除了字尾有 s 外，更重要的是，它們都以 ics 結尾，如 physics、mathematics、mechanics、optics（光學）、acoustics（聲學）、politics、statistics、economics、linguistics、athletics（體育運動）等。

■ 當然以字尾 ics 來判定是否為一門學科不見完全正確，但正確率還頗高，就算不是一門學科，也是一門技術，如特技飛行（aerobatics）。現在還有一些新的學科，如生物數學（biomathematics）和生物統計學（biometrics），它們是合成字，字首加了代表生物學（biology）的 bio。

「Extra Bonus」

■ 小心不要看到字尾 ics 就以為是接單數動詞的學科名稱，以 academic 為例，作為名詞的 academic 是學術人員的意思，複數形式是字尾加 s，成了 academics，看起來很像學科名稱，其實不是。

5-2 考試一點靈

文 法加油站

- 除了學科外，很多疾病名稱也以 s 結尾，看起來像是複數名詞，其實是要接單數動詞，如 arthritis（關節炎）、bronchitis（支氣管炎）、diabetes（糖尿病）等。
  - The diabetes is a chronic disease.

- News（新聞）雖是複數形式，但與單數動詞連用。不能冠以不定冠詞 a 來表示一則新聞，正確的說法是 a piece of news。
  - I've got good news for you.

- 學科名稱前面不用加定冠詞 the，但該名詞若有學科名稱以外的意義時，還是有加 the 的可能性。如 major in economics（主修經濟學），the economics of the project（這個計畫的經濟狀況）。
  - He is a professor of history at National Taiwan University.

實 ▶ 戰句

❶ **Economics often-----topics like wealth, finance, and banking, resulting in the misconception that economics is all about money, rather than a discipline that helps us understand and interpret trends.**

(A) involves

(B) involve

(C) involving

(D) involved

中譯

　　經濟學經常牽涉財富、金融、及銀行之類主題，因而有人誤以為經濟學就是和錢有關，而不是一個幫助我們了解及詮釋趨勢的學門。

考題最前端

　　答題時還是要先做一下句型分析，很顯然主詞是 economics，頻率副詞 often 通常出現在動詞前面，所以空格裡缺的是一個動詞，後面的受詞 topics 更確認了這一點。若是動詞，就要考慮單複數及時態問題。Economics 在這裡顯然是學科名稱，要和單數動詞連用，而 often 通常表達一種經常性的狀態，動詞現在式的可能性遠大於過去式，所以答案是 involves。

答案：(A)

文 法加油站

■ economy class 和 economics class 有什麼差別？前者是搭飛機時的經濟艙，後者是經濟課，很多人在說經濟艙時經常說成經濟課，不得不小心。

  · The rich man usually flies economy class.

■ 有些學科名稱是以 v-ing 的形式出現，通常會讓人誤以為是動名詞或現在分詞，其實它們就是一個名詞，如 accounting（會計學）、engineering（工程學）、marketing（行銷學）。

  · He received a bachelor degree in accounting from a university.

■ 與學科名稱相關的字如媒體（media），原本應該要接複數動詞，現在卻逐漸被視為單數名詞，即便文法正統人士仍然主張維持傳統。

  · The media are going to be present./The media is going to be present.（兩個句子都對）

實 戰句

❷ In September of last year, a vice president of the corporation wrote a memo to the general manager describing some of the problems in that corporation, using the term-----hoax.

(A) account

(B) accounting

(C) accounted

(D) accounts

中譯

　　去年九月，這家企業的副總裁寫了一份備忘錄給總經理，描述企業內部某些問題，其中用到會計騙局這個術語。

考題最前端

　　這個句子是以主要子句（a vice present…in that corporation）和分詞構句（using the…hoax）所組成，句首的 In September of last year 是修飾整個句子的副詞片語。整個句子的主詞是 a vice president，動詞是 wrote，memo 是直接受詞，the general manager 是間接受詞，describing 是 wrote 的附帶動作，以 v-ing 的形式出現，逗點後面是一分詞構句，補充說明 vice president 寫了些什麼，原來他寫到 accounting hoax 這個詞語。accounting hoax 是 the term 的同位語。

答案：(B)

熟悉對等連接詞

單 元概述

何謂對等連接詞？有何功用？

對等連接詞是連接詞的一種，特點是以對等的關係把單字、片語、子句連結在一起。對等連接詞有 and、but、or、so、for，其中最常見的是 and 和 but。所謂對等，就是連結兩個或兩個以上相互對稱或對比的單字、片語、子句，and 還能連結三個以上的詞語。

6-1 文法修行 Let's Go

Q6 請問你都怎麼記憶對等連接詞？有什麼更快的學習方式嗎？

「HOW」

■ 對等連接詞是大家的好朋友，不但經常看到，還經常用到，次數之多，不熟也得熟。這些連接詞叫做粉絲男孩們（**Fanboys**），它們代表著 for、and、nor、but、or、yet、so 這幾字的字首縮寫，如果記不得有哪些對等連接詞，只要想起粉絲男孩們就 OK。這些男孩中，and 和 but 最為活躍，for 雖然帶頭，但活動力沒那麼旺盛，nor 更為不活躍，or、yet、so 還不錯，也經常出來活動，讓大家看看。

「**Extra Bonus**」

■ And 相當於中文的和、又、並且，but 是但是，or 是否則、或者，nor 是也不，for 是因為、既然，so 是因此、所以。

■ 舉世著名的阿巴合唱團（ABBA）在《舞后》（Dancing Queen）一曲中唱到：You come in to look for a king/Anybody could be that guy/Night is young and the music's high（妳進來找一個王/任何人都可能是他/夜還早且曲正熱）。

■ Night is young 和 the music is young 是分別可以獨立的句子，此時用 and 把兩個句子連接在一起，就構成一種對等關係。兩個句子連接在一起後，第二個句子就能把主詞和 be 動詞縮寫在一起，成了 the music's。

「**Extra Bonus**」

■ 對等連接詞連接兩個獨立子句時，要用逗號把兩個子句分開。

- John is watching TV. His wife Mary is talking on the phone. = John is watching TV, and his wife Mary is talking on the phone.

「HOW」

■ 七個對等連接詞中，and 及 or 能連接兩個或兩個以上的對等詞語，其餘五個連接詞基本上只連接兩個對等詞語。以 for 為例，它所引導出來的句子是在表示前面一個句子的原因，so 所引導出來的句子則是在表達前面一個句子的結果。

■ for 和 so 通常只連接兩個子句，而 and、but、or 除了連接對等的子句外，還有單字和片語，應用的範圍比較廣，因此出現的機率比較高。

「Extra Bonus」

■ And 和 or 連接三個對等的詞語時，要用逗號把第三個詞語分開來。

· Do you go to school on foot, by car, or by bus?

· John, Mary, and Andrew all love music.

6-2 考試一點靈

文 法加油站

■ And 連接兩個對等的詞語時，大多後面接複數動詞，但也有些例外，最常見的是 bread and butter，此時兩樣東西被視為單一的整體，要接單數動詞。

· Time and tide waits for no man.

■ Nor 通常出現在 not、no、never 之後，意思是也不。

· The book is not interesting nor informative.

■ Nor 連接兩個否定的句子時，要用倒裝句。

· Jack does not like homework, nor do I.

實 戰句

❶ Since 1972, there have been about 24 Ebola outbreaks in Africa, including one happening now in the Democratic Republic of the Congo. Nine people have been infected-----three people have died as a result.

(A) but

(B) or

(C) and

(D) so

中譯

　自 1972 年起，非洲約有 24 起伊波拉疫情爆發，包括一起正在剛果民主共和國發生的。九人受到感染，三人因而死亡。

考題最前端

　這個段落由兩個句子組成，第一個句子是複雜句（有著從屬子句、修飾性片語、及補充說明的分詞構句的句子），第二個句子是複合句（由對等連接詞連接起來的兩個或兩個以上獨立子句）。懂得這些句型的同學應該很快看出第二個句子是個複合句，對等連接詞才能連接兩個各自獨立的子句（各有主詞和動詞）。答案選項中只有 and 最符合，因為兩個子句相互連貫，不是在表達對立的概念。

答案：(C)

文 法加油站

■ 簡單句是最簡單的句型，只有主詞和述詞，複合句是兩個或兩個以上的簡單句組合而成，這些簡單句通常由對等連接詞連接起來。

· Peter wrote a business proposal, and his boss liked it very much.

■ 也可以不用對等連接詞來連接兩個獨立子句，只要在兩個句子間加入一分號（semicolon）即可。

· The teacher came in late; he forgot to do a roll call.

■ 兩個簡單句間若是用到承轉詞（moreover、however、therefore、nevertheless、in fact、on the other hand），就要用分號來加以連接，而不是對等連接詞。

· Paul missed the first bus; however, he reached office on time.

實 戰句

❷ **People who support the proposal to levy taxes on sugar-sweetened beverages say this plan will reduce obesity-----that consumers will look for healthier alternatives. But there are doubts about whether the taxation will really change consumer behavior.**

(A) and

(B) so

(C) but

(D) or

中譯

　　支持含糖飲料稅提案的人說這個計畫將減少肥胖且消費者會去尋找比較健康的替代選項。但還是有人質疑這種課稅機制能否真的改變消費者行為。

考題最前端

　　這題考一個比較難的句型，即 people（they）say that 這個句型。通常 say 後面只會接一個 that 子句，但也可以有兩個 that 子句，此時第一個 that 子句的 that 可以去掉，但第二個 that 子句的 that 一定要保留，而兩個 that 子句之間就用 and 連結。可能有人會選 so，以為要套用 so that 這個句型，因為文法上沒錯，可是意義上不通。

答案：(A)

了解定冠詞

何謂定冠詞？有何功用？

定冠詞就是 *the*，放在單複數可數名詞和不可數名詞前面表示「這個」或「這些」，意思和不定冠詞 *a/an* 不同，如 *a table* 是一張桌子，*the table* 是某特定的桌子，*the tables* 是多張的特定桌子，*tables* 則泛指任何的多張桌子。

另外，第一次提到某張桌子時，我們會說 *a table*，等到聽者知道我們在說哪張桌子時，就可以說 *the table*。

7-1 文法修行 Let's Go

Q7 請問你都怎麼記憶定冠詞？有什麼更快的學習方式嗎？

「HOW」

■ 什麼時候要加定冠詞？情況很多，無法一言以蔽之，只能挑幾個最明顯的來說。首先，獨一無二的東西要加 the，如 the earth、the sun、the moon、the sky、the world 等，或是指唯一的人，如 He's the one person who can help you. 除了獨一無二外，形容詞的最高級也要加 the，如 the best、the oldest、the most beautiful、the most intelligent 等。

■ 另外，某些字前面一定要加 the，這些字包括 only、sole、same、first、second、last、next、following 等。

「**Extra Bonus**」

■ The 後面的名詞如果是以子音或半母音起始，the 要發成 [ðə]，如 the plane。

■ 如果名詞是以母音起始，the 要唸成 [ðɪ]。

「HOW」

■ 傻瓜花園（Fool's Garden）在《檸檬樹》（Lemon Tree）一曲中唱到：I wonder how, I wonder why yesterday you told me/'Bout the blue blue sky and all that I can see is just/A yellow lemon tree. I'm turning my head up and down/（我想知道如何，我想知道為什麼昨天你告訴我/有關藍藍的天，而我只看到/一棵黃色檸檬樹/我的頭上下點著）。

■ the blue blue sky 是藍藍的天，天空為一獨一無二的實體存在，前面要加 the，至於連續用兩個相同的形容詞 blue 來形容 sky，是詩詞歌曲中才會出現的修辭技巧。

「Extra Bonus」

■ 《檸檬樹》還有另一段歌詞：I'm sitting here, I miss the power, I'd like to go out（我坐在這裡，我懷念著權力，我想要出去），power 指權力時要加 the，表示電力時通常不加 the。

「**HOW**」

■ The 後面通常接名詞，也有接形容詞，如形容詞的最高級和 only、same 之類的特定字，除此之外，還有接某些形容詞來表達特定一群人或民族，如 the French = the French people，the Chinese = the Chinese people, the rich = the rich people，the old = the old people。

■ 這種詞語很獨特，很好辨識，如果不確定是不是在說一群人，只要試著用什麼 people 的方式來表達，如果通，就沒錯。如 the young，如果可以用 the young people 的方式來表達，就是對的。如果不行，則是錯的。

「**Extra Bonus**」

■ 用 the 加形容詞的方式來表達一群人，一定要搭配複數動詞，既然是一群人，就不可能用單數動詞。

・ The French are famous for their cuisines.

1-2 考試一點靈

文 法加油站

■ 河流、海洋、群島、山脈、沙漠、盆地、運河、海峽、海灣等地理名稱前面要加 the。

- An American from the Rocky Mountains sailed across the Pacific Ocean in a boat. He reached the Philippine Islands.

■ 複數形式的地名、國名、姓氏、隊名，如 the Netherlands、the United States、the Browns、the Chicago Bulls。

- The Chicago Bulls is one of the best professional basketball teams in the United States.

■ 國名中有 kingdom、union、republic 等字，要冠上 the。如 the United Kingdom、the Republic of Ireland、the Czech Republic。

- The United Kingdom of Great Britain and Northern Island is commonly known as the United Kingdom.

實 戰句

❶ **Earlier studies into associations between coffee consumption and type 2 diabetes showed that people drinking at least 7 cups of coffee per day were half as likely to develop type 2 diabetes. -----association was statistically significant.**

(A) A

(B) An

(C) The

(D) X

中譯

　　早先針對喝咖啡與第二型糖尿病間關係所做的研究顯示，一天喝至少 7 杯咖啡的人得第二型糖尿病的機率只有一般人的一半。這樣的關連性在統計學上具有重要意義。

考題最前端

　　此句主詞是 earlier studies 後面 into... diabetes 是修飾主詞的形容詞片語，動詞是 showed，that 子句中的主詞是 people，後面 drinking... per day 是修飾 people 的分詞片語，動詞是 were，後面跟著主詞補語。第二句是個簡單句，主詞 association 之前要接個冠詞，由於前句提到咖啡和糖尿病間的關係，所以要用 the 來表示這個提過的 association。

答案：(C)

文 法加油站

■ 大型建築物前面要加 the，如 the Statue of Liberty、the Great Wall of China、the Great Pyramid。

· It was once widely believed that the Great Wall of China can be seen from the space.

■ 報刊名稱前面要加 the，如 the Times、the New York Times, the China Post、the Taipei Times。

· The New York Times is an American daily newspaper founded in 1851.

■ 大範圍區域，如 the Middle East、the Far East。

· The Middle East is known as the cradle of civilization.

實 戰句

❷ **As we become more health-conscious, there has been an increased focus on----- importance of exercise. Exercise and stress management are closely linked. An office worker can use exercise as an effective stress reliever.**

(A) an

(B) a

(C) this

(D) the

中譯

隨著我們越來越有健康意識，對運動的重要性也益發關注。運動和壓力管理之間有著密切的關連性。上班族可以把運動當成一種有效的紓壓方式。

考題最前端

這一題用到複雜句句型，也就是由主要子句和附屬子句構成的句子，這裡的附屬子句是由 as 所引導的副詞子句，副詞子句可以放句首或句尾，這裡是放句首。主要子句中的 there 是假主詞，真主詞是 focus，後面 on 所引導的片語是在修飾 focus，作為 on 的受詞，importance 需要一個冠詞來連接 on，此時只能用定冠詞 the。

答案：(D)

了解不定冠詞

單 元概述

　　何謂不定冠詞？有何功用？

　　英文的不定冠詞只有兩個，即 a 和 an，不是用 a 就是用 an，指的是任何一個非特定的單數可數名詞，定冠詞 the 則是指特定的「那一個」。什麼時候使用 a，什麼時候使用 an？很簡單，後面單字若第一個字母是子音發音，就用 a，字首是 u 和 eu（唸起來像是 you）的單字也要接 a。若字首是母音發音（a、e、i、o、u）或不發音的 h，就要用 an。

8-1 文法修行 Let's Go

Q8 請問你都怎麼記憶不定冠詞？有什麼更快的學習方式嗎？

「HOW」

■ 不定冠詞簡單來說就是用來指稱某個第一次提到的人或事物，如 a man、a tiger、an accident、an orange、an FBI agent、a historic event、an hour 等。是指任何一個 man、tiger 或 accident。第一次提用不定冠詞，第二次提則要用定冠詞 the，例如：A traffic accident happened yesterday. Two people were injured in the accident. 是不是很簡單！不過有些字要小心，像是 man，當可數名詞時指男人，複數是 men，當不可數名詞時則指人類，不可加冠詞，如 the history of man。

「Extra Bonus」

■ 不定冠詞除了用來指第一次提到的東西，還可表示數量，如 a drink、an orange，但不可數名詞則不可用不定冠詞來表示數量，如果一定要表示數量，不同不可數名詞有不同的表示方式，如 a loaf of bread、a piece of paper、a bottle of milk 等。

「HOW」

■ 路易斯‧阿姆斯壯（Louis Armstrong）在《美好世界》（What a wonderful world）一曲中唱到：I see trees of green, red roses too/I see them bloom for me and you/And I think to myself what a wonderful world.（我看到綠色的樹，還有紅玫瑰/我看到它們為我和你開花/我心中想著這是一個多麼美好的世界）。

■ What 所引導的驚嘆句要在名詞之前加不定冠詞 a 或 an，如 What a beautiful girl your sister is!，這類句子通常在句尾要加驚嘆號！但也有人不加。

「Extra Bonus」

■ What 所引導的感嘆句也可改為 how+形容詞+不定冠詞+名詞的句型，例如：What a beautiful girl your sister is! = How beautiful a girl your sister is!記得 how 要先接形容詞再接不定冠詞。

「**HOW**」

■ 不定冠詞 a/an 在表示數量時和 one 有何差別？不少人會搞錯。舉例來說，Give me a pen. 和 Give me one pen. 在文法上都對，但前者是說給我一支筆，任何一種都可以，後者是說給我一支筆，強調一支就好。

■ 有人問 How many pens do you have? 你只有一支，回答時要說 Only one，而不是 a。不過 a/an 和 one 有時候是可以互通，指的是某一個，例如：A Mr. Wang called you. 和 One Mr. Wang called you. 意思一樣，都是「某個王先生打電話給你」。

「**Extra Bonus**」

■ 某些慣用語用 a/an 或 one 都 OK，可以彼此互換，例如：at a/one stroke（一舉）、in a/one word（一句話）、not for a/one moment（絕不）。

1-2 考試一點靈

文 法加油站

■ 不定冠詞可用來表達一種身份、職業、或群體的一部份。如 a doctor、an engineer、a teacher。

・You must study hard to become a doctor.

■ 不定冠詞可用來表達國籍或宗教信仰。如 an Englishman、an American、a Catholic 等。

・As a Buddhist, Mr. Lin often donates money to help the poor.

■ 不定冠詞放在星期一到星期日名稱前是表示任何的那一天。

・I met her on a Sunday.

實 戰句

❶ **What is the difference between humans and animals? The classic question continues to puzzle many people as a new century has arrived. -----recent book now provides an answer that is both scientific and religious.**

(A) The

(B) A

(C) An

(D) X

中譯

　　人類和動物有何差異？這個經典問題在新世紀來臨之際持續困惑著許多人。現在一本新近出版的書提供了一個既科學又符合宗教意義的解釋。

考題最前端

　　這段文字中的句子都很簡單，考題明顯在測驗考生對冠詞的理解，看是要放定冠詞還是不定冠詞，有人會選定冠詞 the，以為是在接續前面提過的名詞，事實上，這裡所提的是一本書，前面根本沒有說任何書，只有提到 the classic question，這個經典問題是「人類和動物有何差異？」。一本最近出版的書為這個問題提供了答案。answer 後面的 that 子句是用來修飾 answer 的形容詞子句。

答案：(B)

文 法加油站

■ 數字 8、與 8 相關的數字、及數字 11 的字首都是以母音發音，要用 an。如 an eight-hour workday、an 11-year-old boy。

  · John is an 18-year-old boy who likes to play basketball.

■ 字母 f、h、l、m、n、r、s、x 都是母音發音，以這些字母構成的縮寫字也要用 an。如 an MBA degree、an X-ray image。

  · Mary considers going to business school to get an MAB degree.

■ H 有時發音有時不發音，子音發音時，單字前面接 a，若是不發音，單字前面就要接 an，因為不發音的 h 讓後面的母音直接面對不定冠詞。如 an hour、a historic event。

  · They observed a historic event an hour ago.

實 戰句

❷ NASA's flying observatory, the Stratospheric Observatory for Infrared Astronomy, recently completed a detailed study of-----nearby planetary system. The study confirmed that this nearby planetary system is similar our solar system.

(A) the

(B) an

(C) a

(D) x

中譯

　　美國太空總署稱為紅外線天文學同溫層天文台的飛行天文台最近完成一項針對一個鄰近行星系統所做的仔細研究，此項研究證實這個鄰近的行星系統類似我們的太陽系。

考題最前端

　　這段文章的第一個句子看似複雜，事實上就是主詞+動詞+受詞的句型，主詞是 NASA's flying observatory，後面用逗號分開來的 Stratospheric Observatory for Infrared Astronomy 是主詞的同位語，recently 是修飾動詞 completed 的副詞，a detailed study 是受詞，由 of 引導出來的片語是修飾 study 的形容詞片語。把結構搞清楚後，就可以知道空格裡缺的是一個冠詞，由於這套行星系統沒有被提過，是第一次出現，所以要用 a

答案：(C)

主詞動詞的一致性

單 元概述

何謂主詞動詞的一致性？如何達到一致性？

一言以蔽之，單數主詞搭配單數動詞，複數主詞搭配複數動詞，問題是，有時候搞不清楚所面對的主詞是單數還是複數，因為主詞後面加了一些形容詞片語或補充說明的詞語，讓讀者誤以為是複數，其實還是單數。另外，部分集合名詞有時接單數動詞有時接複數動詞，也常讓人感到困擾，但也沒那麼難，習慣它們就好。

9-1 文法修行 Let's Go

Q9 請問你都怎麼記憶主詞動詞的一致性？有什麼更快的學習方式嗎？

「HOW」

■ 後面接介係詞片語的主詞常常被誤以為是複數，我就來為大家釋疑一下。以 Each of them has a pen. 這個句子為例，each 是主詞，of them 是修飾主詞的介係詞片語，不影響主詞的單複數。可是有人舉 a group of 為例說主詞不是 group，怎麼動詞還用複數動詞？很簡單，a group of 是一個計量詞語，真正的主詞在後面，如 A group of people have come. 同類的詞語還有 a number of、a couple of、a lot of、the majority of、half of，這些詞語就是要這麼說，後面的 of 不是在引導一個介係詞片語。

「**Extra Bonus**」

■ A number of 表達一些數量後面接複數主詞和複數動詞，可是 the number of 卻不一樣，要接單數動詞。例如：A number of students are sick.表示一些學生生病了，The number of students getting sick is on the rise.表示生病學生的數目在上升，此時 of students getting sick 是修飾 number 的介係詞片語。

「HOW」

■ 蘇珊·薇佳（Suzanne Vega）在《湯姆小館》（Tom's Diner）一曲中唱到：I am sitting/In the morning/At the diner/On the corner/I am waiting/At the counter/For the man/To pour the coffee/…/"It is always/Nice to see you"/Says the man/Behind the counter.（早晨的我/坐在/角落的/小館/我在櫃臺/等著/那人/倒咖啡…/「見到妳/總是很很高興」/櫃臺後的/男人說著）。

■ It is always nice to see you.這個句子以 it 為虛主詞，不定詞片語 to see you 為主詞，所以動詞是第三人稱單數。

「Extra Bonus」

■ It is+被強調部分+that 子句也是一種常見的句型。例如：It was they that/who cleaned the classroom yesterday.被強調部分可以是主詞、受詞、或副詞，It was the classroom that they cleaned yesterday.強調的是教室，It was yesterday that they cleaned the classroom.強調的是昨天。

Part I 基礎實力養成篇

Part II 進階文法修練篇

「HOW」

■ 主詞後面如果跟著 with、together with、including、accompanied by、in addition to、或 as well，動詞的單複數還是要看主詞本身，不受這些詞語的影響，但主詞和它們之間要用逗號分開。例如：The President, accompanied by his wife, is travelling to Japan. 這個句子的主詞是 President，accompanied by his wife 是補充說明的詞語，補充說明的東西一定要用逗號分開，這樣才能一目了然。

■ Nervousness, as well as ill health, is the cause of her shaking. 同樣地，as well as ill health 也是補充說明，不影響主詞 nervousness 的單數。

「Extra Bonus」

■ 另外要提到的是，如果 as well as 沒有被逗號分開，而是和另一個主詞並列，此時的功能相當於對等連接詞 and，動詞通常就要用複數動詞。

　・His appearance as well as his way of talking make people laugh.

9-2 考試一點靈

文 法加油站

■ 主詞之間如果用 or、either/or、neither/nor 來連接，動詞單複數取決於最靠近動詞的那個主詞。

· Neither she nor her children have arrived.

■ 主詞後如果有括弧，括弧內的詞語不是主詞的一部分。

· Mr. Lin（John's father）was arrested by the police.

■ There is/are 的句型中，由於 there 是假主詞，真主詞在後面，be 動詞的單複數要看主詞的單複數而定。

· There are several difficult tasks to handle.

■ 當一段距離和時間或一筆金額被看成一整體時，動詞要用單數。

· Ten kilometers is a long distance.

實 戰句

❶ **Researchers analyzed surveys completed separately by mothers and fathers, who were asked about their use of smartphones, tablets, laptops, and other devices and how-----devices disrupted their family time, such as in**

the form of checking phone messages during the time they were supposed to play with their children.

(A) x

(B) a

(C) the

(D) an

中譯

　　研究人員分析父母分開來做的問卷，這些父母被問到他們使用智慧型手機、平板電腦、筆電、及其他裝置的情形，以及這些裝置如何打斷他們的家庭時間，像是在應該與小孩玩樂的時間查看電話上的訊息。

考題最前端

　　整段文字就是一個句子，主詞是 researchers，動詞是 analyzed，受詞是 surveys，後面的 completed separately by mothers and fathers 是修飾 surveys 的分詞片語，這個分詞片語裡的 mothers and fathers 又被一個由 who 引導的形容詞子句形容，who 是主格關係代名詞，動詞是被動式 were asked，被問到的事情有兩樣，一是 3C 產品的使用情形，另一是這些裝置如何打斷他們的家庭時間。由於前面提過 3C 裝置，後面再提就用 the devices 來代替。

答案：(C)

文 法加油站

■ 表示部分或整體的詞語，如 a lot、a majority、some、all，後面接單數名詞，動詞就用單數，複數名詞就用複數動詞。

  · A lot of the pie has been eaten./A lot of the pies have been eaten.

■ None 應該接單數動詞才對，但也有接複數動詞。

  · None of them play（s）basketball.

■ 集合名詞如 group、team、committee、class、family 被視為一整體，要接單數動詞。

  · The team practices for a running contest.

實 戰句

❷ **Smart phones have gradually become the storage place for-----details that drive our everyday lives, but researchers have recently discovered that our information has been secretly stolen by the apps we regularly use on our phones.**

(A) few

(B) many

(C) x

(D) the

中譯

　　智慧型手機逐漸變成我們日常生活大小事的儲藏庫，但研究人員最近發現，我們的訊息正悄悄地被我們常用的手機應用軟體盜走。

考題最前端

　　這段文字是由 but 所連接的兩個對等子句構成，第一個子句的主詞是 smart phones，動詞是完成式連綴動詞 have become，storage place 是主詞補語，後面的 for the details that drive our daily lives 是修飾 storage place 的介系詞片語，而 that 所引導的句子則是修飾 details 的形容詞子句，這些 details 是特定的 details，是驅動我們日常生活的 details，所以要用 the。

答案：(D)

區分動詞單、複數

單 元概述

何謂動詞單、複數？如何區別？

動詞現在式的單、複數變化比較複雜，過去式簡單多了，單數用 was，複數用 were。動詞現在式還要看人稱來做變化，第一人稱單數主詞 I 接 be 動詞時 be 動詞要變化成 am，接一般動詞時一般動詞為動詞的原形，以下列出各個人稱的動詞單、複數變化：I am/I do; we are/we do; you are/you do; he (she) is/he (she) does; they are/they do。

10-1 文法修行 Let's Go

Q10 請問你都怎麼記憶動詞單、複數？有什麼更快的學習方式嗎？

「**HOW**」

■ 要搞清楚動詞單、複數變化，首先必須把人稱代名詞弄懂。以一般動詞來說，只有第三人稱單數主詞才要在動詞後面加 s、es、ies，第一人稱和第二人稱單、複數主詞都接動詞原形。

■ be 動詞的變化比較複雜一點，第一人稱單數主詞的 be 動詞形式 am 是獨一無二的，另外兩個 be 動詞形式 is 和 are，就可以涵蓋其他人稱單、複數主詞的 be 動詞變化，先記住這些要領就可以慢慢搞清楚。

「**Extra Bonus**」

■ 還有一個常用的 have 動詞，其原形適用於第一人稱單、複數主詞、第二人稱單、複數主詞、第三人稱複數主詞，只有第三人稱單數主詞（he、she、it）用 has。

■ 用一首歌曲來解釋會比較好了解。金屬製品樂團（Metallica）在《其他都不重要》（Nothing else matters）一曲中唱到：I never opened myself this way/Life is ours, we live it our way/All these words I don't just say/And nothing else matters.（我從沒這麼放開自己/生命是我們的，我們用我們的方式過活/我不是只是說說/而其他都不重要）。

■ 不定代名詞 nothing 為第三人稱單數主詞，所以要用單數動詞。Else 慣用於不定代名詞之後，表示其他、另外。

「**Extra Bonus**」

■ 除了 nothing，不定代名詞還有 anything、everything、something、nothing，它們屬於第三人稱單數主詞，要用單數動詞。但不是所有的不定代名詞都接單數動詞。像 many 就要接複數動詞，因為就等於 many people。

「HOW」

■ 複數動詞經常是動詞的原形,沒太大的變化,可是第三人稱單數主詞的動詞卻是變化多多,要特別注意才行。

Part I 基礎實力養成篇

Part II 進階文法修練篇

■ 這些變化有幾類:大部分動詞後面加 s 即可,如 eat→eats,play→plays,sleep→sleeps;字尾是 s、sh、ch、z、x、o 的動詞要加 es,如 teach→teaches,wash→washes,kiss→kisses,do→does;字尾是子音加 y 的動詞要去 y 加 ies,如 study→studies,apply→applies,cry→cries;have→has。

「Extra Bonus」

■ 不過如果字尾是母音+y,動詞只用加 s。

・ buy→buys,obey→obeys,enjoy→enjoys。

10-2 考試一點靈

文 法加油站

■ 名詞的單複數變化類似動詞，沒有特殊情況加 s 就好，如 girl→girls，dog→dogs，book→books。這些名詞變複數後接複數動詞（大多和動詞原形一樣）。

· The girls like roses./The girl likes roses.

■ 單字字尾是 s、z、sh、ch、x 時要加上 es，如 bus→buses，glass→glasses，dish→dishes，watch→watches。

· There are some watches for you to choose from.

■ 單字字尾是子音 + y 時要去 y 加上 ies，如 city→cities，baby→babies，cherry→cherries。

· Many cities in the world have air pollution problems.

實 戰句

❶ **A medical student tries out a device that-----electrical activity in his hand and leads his hand to open and close in response to brain signals, a new study which indicates post-stroke patients can regain some control over their paralyzed limbs using the device.**

(A) detects

(B) detect

(C) detected

(D) detectes

中譯

　　一名醫學院學生測試一項能偵測到他手部電流活動並促使其根據大腦訊號做出打開閉合動作的裝置，這項新研究顯示中風後患者可以用這個裝置恢復癱瘓四肢的部分控制能力。

考題最前端

　　這個句子有一個單數主詞 medical student，動詞是 try out，try 的字尾是子音加 y，必須去 y 加 ies，成了 tries。動詞的受詞是 device，device 後面跟著一個由 that 引導的形容詞子句，這個形容詞子句修飾 device，關係代名詞為主格，後面直接接動詞，由於先行詞 device 是單數，必須用單數動詞。只要在 detect 後面加 s，就變成第三人稱單數動詞。

答案：(A)

Part
I
基礎實力養成篇

Part
II
進階文法修練篇

■ 單字字尾是 o 時要加 s / es，如 hero→heroes，potato→potatoes，zoo→zoos，piano→pianos。動詞時則是 es，如 go→goes，do→does。

- Potatoes grow outdoors.

■ 碰到疑問句，就要用上 do 和 does，第一和第二人稱單數主詞及所有人稱的複數主詞用 do 構成疑問句，第三人稱單數主詞用 does 構成疑問句。

- Do you like beer? /Does Jack like to play baseball?

■ 否定句時，第一、第二人稱單數主詞及所有人稱的複數主詞要用 do not（don't），第三人稱單數主詞則用 does not（doesn't）。

- They do not drink coffee./Mr. Lin doesn't play golf.

實 戰句

❷ **An analysis based on existing studies that investigated more than 3.5 million people in more than 90 countries found out that depression-----far more females than males, showing that depression mainly, but not entirely, affects women.**

(A) affects

(B) affect

(C) affected

(D) effect

中譯

　　一份根據調查過 90 多個國家 350 多萬人的現存研究所做的分析報告發現，抑鬱症對女性的影響遠超過男性，顯示抑鬱症主要地但不全然地影響女性。

考題最前端

　　這一句子就是主詞 an analysis+動詞 confirmed+that 子句+分詞構句的句型，based on existing studies 是修飾主詞的分詞片語，這個片語中又有一個修飾 studies、由 that 所引導的形容詞子句。空格位於 confirmed 後面的 that 子句，裡面 depression 是主詞，後面缺的顯然是個動詞，問題在於單數還是負數，現在式還是過去式。Depression 是不可數名詞，而講述的是研究成果，必須用現在式。

答案：(A)

熟悉頻率副詞

單 元概述

何謂頻率副詞？有何功用？

頻率副詞又稱次數副詞，表示事情發生的頻率，常用的有 always（總是）、usually（通常）、often（時常）、normally/generally（正常地，一般地）、frequently（頻繁地）、sometimes（有時地）、occasionally（偶爾地）、rarely/seldom（不常）、ever（從來）、never（從不）、daily/every day（每天）、once（一次）。

頻率副詞通常擺在一般動詞前面，be 動詞和助動詞的後面。

11-1 文法修行 Let's Go

Q11 請問你都怎麼記憶頻率副詞？有什麼更快的學習方式嗎？

「**HOW**」

■ 若按照事件的發生頻率來看，100%的發生率是 always，90%的發生率是 usually，80%的發生率是 normally/generally，70%的發生率是 often/frequently、50%的發生率是 sometimes，30%的發生率是 occasionally，10%的發生率是 seldom，5%的發生率是 hardly ever/rarely，0%的發生率是 never。

■ Always 和 never 是兩個極端，中間則有多種表達不同程度發生率的頻率副詞。至於 every day、once a month、twice a year、three times a day、every other week 這些頻率副詞，則明確地表達出發生的次數。

「**Extra Bonus**」

■ 明確地表達次數的副詞還有 hourly、daily、weekly、monthly、yearly、every second、once a minute、once、twice、three times 等。

「HOW」

■ 搖滾樂團邦喬飛（Bon Jovi）在《總是》（Always）這一首歌中唱到：It's been raining since you left me/Now I'm drowning in the flood/You see I've always been a fighter/But without you I give up.（妳離開我後就在下雨/我淹沒在洪水中/妳看我一直是個戰士/但沒了妳我會放棄）。

■ I have always been a fighter.表達是一種持續的狀態，很少人會說 I am usually a fighter. 或 I am occasionally a fighter.這樣聽起來很可笑，要當 fighter 就要一直當下去，沒有偶爾當當這一回事。

「Extra Bonus」

■ 如果用 always 來表示一種持續的狀態或本來就擁有的能力，要搭配現在完成式。

- People have always had the ability to create.

「HOW」

■ 頻率副詞除了放句中外，還可放句首，但有些可放句首，有些不能放。我們來看看。可放句首的頻率副詞有 usually、normally、often、frequently、sometimes、occasionally。例如：

Occasionally, I like to eat Japanese food.

■ 但 always、seldom、rarely、ever、never 等頻率副詞不能放句首，除非改為倒裝句，seldom、rarely、never 這種否定副詞可放句首形成倒裝句，例如：Seldom does he go to work by bus. 不過 always 和 ever 不管在什麼情況都無法放句首，這是沒辦法改的。

「Extra Bonus」

■ Ever 通常用在疑問句和否定句中。

· Have you ever been to Canada?

· I haven't ever been to Sweden.

11-2 考試一點靈

文 法加油站

■ 頻率副詞出現在一般動詞之前。

· I always remember to get up early.

■ 碰到 be 動詞，頻率副詞就在放在後面。

· She is usually late for work.

■ 如果有助動詞，頻率副詞要放在助動詞和一般動詞之間。

· You can sometimes give us a ride.

實 戰句

❶ Behind the seeming randomness of a basketball game, there is a self-organization process going on amid the teams. The interactions between team mates and their opponents are-----influencing each other.

(A) seldom

(B) rarely

(C) constantly

(D) ever

中譯

在籃球看似雜亂無章的背後，隊伍之間正出現一個自我組織的過程。隊員及對手之間的互動不斷地相互影響著。

考題最前端

這段文字有兩個句子，第一個句子先以複詞片語（behind the apparent randomness of a basketball game）開場，主要子句是 there is 句型，主詞是 a process，of self-organization 則為修飾 process 的介係詞片語，後面的 taking place amid the teams 是分詞片語，修飾前面的 a process of self-organization。第二個句子的主詞是 interactions，動詞是 are influencing，可以放到 be 動詞和現在分詞之間的是副詞，而這個副詞應非否定副詞，而是正面的表述，答案只有 constantly 符合。

答案：(C)

文 法加油站

- 頻率副詞中的 hourly、daily、weekly、yearly、once a minute、twice 都具有固定的頻率，這種固定頻率副詞通常在句尾。
  - The old man goes to the doctor once a week.

- 有時固定頻率副詞也可放在句首作為強調之用。
  - Every day，thousands of people die on the road.

- 有一些常用的頻率副詞片語，如 as usual、as always、as is often the case、just like always
  - You look great, as usual.

實 戰句

❷ As is--the case with an attractive woman, his wife's defect—the shortness of her upper lip—seems to become her own special form of beauty. In other words, she is attractive in her own way.

(A) weekly

(B) seldom

(C) often

(D) never

中譯

　　就像迷人女子常有的狀況，琳達的缺陷，亦即上嘴唇的短小，似乎成了她的一種獨特的美。換句話說，她的迷人之處自成一格。

考題最前端

　　as is often the case with 是一種慣用語，把 often 換成 always 也可以。這個片語在句首作為副詞片語，主詞是 defect，後面破折號所引導出來的 the shortness of her upper lip 相當於 defect 的同為語，意思是缺陷就是 the shortness of her upper lip。慣用語 in other words 引導出第二句，補充説明她具有的是一種自成一格的吸引力。

答案：(C)

熟悉情態副詞

單 元概述

何謂情態副詞？有何功用？

情態副詞又稱方式副詞，用來說明事情進行的方式（how），或動作發生時的情形或狀態。這類副詞通常以 ly 結尾，放在動詞或動詞片語之後。常見的有 carefully、closely、correctly、safely、slowly、easily、well、loudly、badly、hard、fast、happily、kindly、naturally、patiently、politely、quickly 等。

12-1 文法修行 Let's Go

Q12 請問你都怎麼記憶情態副詞？有什麼更快的學習方式嗎？

「**HOW**」

■ 情態動詞通常以 ly 結尾，但有些例外，像 hard、fast、well，但畢竟是少數。情態副詞通常有替代的說法，如 He drives slowly. =He is a slow driver. 他開得很慢就等於他是一個慢速駕駛，中文比較沒有這種替代說法，開得很慢就是開得很慢。英文的這種替代說法除了表達情態副詞的特性，也多提供一種修辭上的選項，這是英文的一個長處。再舉一個例子，He works carefully. =He is a careful worker.

「**Extra Bonus**」

■ Fast 和 hard 也可做以上的替換，例如：He works hard. =He is a hard worker. 或 She runs fast.=She is fast runner. 但不是所有的狀況都可以做這樣的替換。另外，well 無法做修飾名詞的形容詞，只能當副詞。例如：He sings well.不能用 He is a well singer.來代替，這是錯誤的句子，要改成 He is a good singer.才對。

「**HOW**」

■ Fugees 樂團在《溫柔地要了我的命》（Killing Me Softly）這首歌中唱到：Strumming my pain with his fingers,/Singing my life with his words,/Killing me softly with his song/（他用手指彈奏出我的痛/用他的話唱出我的生命/溫柔地要了我的命）。

■ 這裡的 softly 就是一個情態副詞，只能擺在動詞的受詞 me 後面，不能說成 Softly killing me... 或 Killing me with his song softly.情境副詞在放在動詞的直接受詞後面，如 She ate the cake greedily.一般不會說成 She greedily ate the cake.但為了強調 greedily 這個狀態，也可以這麼說。

「**Extra Bonus**」

■ Softly 也可以用 in a soft manner 這個副詞片語來代替，但很少人會這麼用，因為比較麻煩，softly 簡潔有力，為何不用？許多其他情態副詞也可用 in a…manner 來代替，如 gently = in a gentle manner。

「HOW」

■ 確切地來說，情態副詞在動詞為不及物動詞時放在動詞的後面，當動詞為及物動詞時則放在受詞的後面。例如：He swims well.（情態副詞 well 放在不及物動物 swim 之後），She considered the option carefully.（情態副詞 carefully 放在及物動詞 consider 的受詞 option 之後）。

■ 大多數狀況都是如此，但情態副詞也可放在動詞的前面，如第二個例句可改為 She carefully considered the option. 以強調 carefully 這個狀態，但第一個例句就不可改為 He well swims，這是錯誤的句子。

「Extra Bonus」

■ 歸納起來，不管是及物還是不及物動詞，只要動詞後面沒有受詞，情態副詞就要放在動詞後面。

· The city grew quickly.

12-2 考試一點靈

文 法加油站

■ 如果動詞後面有介系詞，情態副詞可以放在介系詞之前或介系詞的受詞之後。

- The young man ran happily toward his girlfriend. /The young man ran toward his girlfriend happily.

■ 有些情態副詞幾乎一定放在動詞後面，如 well、badly、hard、fast。

- He treats people badly.

■ 有助動詞時，情態副詞要放在助動詞和動詞之間，被動語態則要放在過去分詞之前，be 動詞之後。

- You should carefully examine the case./The case should be carefully examined by you.

實 戰句

❶ **Donald Trump's surprise win in the United States presidential election was considered by many people to indicate that election polling is no longer effective, but some researchers claim they have developed models that can-----predict election outcomes.**

(A) good

(B) correctly

(C) correct

(D) carefully

中譯

　　川普意外當選美國總統在許多人看來代表著選舉民調不再有效，但有些研究人員宣稱他們開發出可以正確地預測選舉結果的模式。

考題最前端

　　這段文字由 but 所連接的兩個對等子句構成，第二個句子的主詞是 some researchers，動詞是 say，後面跟著 that 所引導的名詞子句，名詞子句中的主詞是 they，動詞是 have developed，受詞是 models，後面 that 所引導的是修飾 models 的形容詞子句，此時 that 是主格關係代名詞，後面直接接動詞。助動詞和動詞之間可以放副詞，所以答案是 correctly。

答案：(B)

文 法加油站

■ 情態副詞有時也可放在句首。其中一個狀況是為了強調。

　・Slowly she picked up the book.

■ 情態副詞放在句首時，如果不是為了強調，就是一個附加的修飾語，
　表達對整個句子的看法或評論，此時要在副詞後面加逗號。
　He did the thing foolishly.的意思不同於 Foolishly, he did the thing.

■ 文藝作家經常把情態副詞擺在句首，都是為了強調情態副詞所具有的
　意義。

　・Slowly, carefully, she opened the letter.

實 戰句

❷ U.S. Secretary of State Hilary Clinton's announcement that Washington will begin talks with Cuba on bilateral migration issues indicates that the Obama administration plans to proceed-----toward normalizing relations with Cuba.

(A) immediately

(B) cautiously

(C) silently

(D) quietly

中譯

　　美國國務卿希拉蕊宣布華盛頓將與古巴就兩國人民相互往來議題展開談話，這暗示了歐巴馬總統政府計畫朝與古巴關係正常化的目標審慎地邁進。

考題最前端

　　這個句子比較複雜一點，裡面用到兩個 that 子句，但這兩個 that 子句不一樣。第一個 that 子句是 announcement 的同位語，為一名詞子句，而第二個 that 子句則是動詞 suggests 後面的名詞子句。整個句子的主詞是 Hilary's announcement，動詞是 suggests，後面的 that 名詞子句是受詞，子句裡的主詞是 President Barack Obama's administration，動詞是 plans，後面接不定詞 to proceed toward，顯然中間缺一個副詞，只有 cautiously 最符合句意。

答案：(B)

副詞的位置

單 元概述

副詞的位置怎麼放呢？有何訣竅？

副詞的位置有句首、句中、及句尾，放在句首和句尾比較簡單，因為只要用逗號把副詞和句子的其他部分隔開，不用擔心要在哪些詞語的前面還是後面。放在句中就要記住是在助動詞之後，助動詞和動詞之間，動詞之後，及形容詞之前，聽起來很複雜，多看一些例句就清楚了。

13-1 文法修行 Let's Go

Q13 請問你都怎麼記憶副詞的位置？有什麼更快的學習方式嗎？

「HOW」

■ 副詞有好幾種：情態副詞、時間副詞、地方副詞、頻率副詞、程度副詞、目的副詞、時間副詞等。它們可以擺放的位置不外乎句首、句中、及句尾，其中又以時間副詞和地方副詞的位置比較固定，時間副詞（recently、now、then、yesterday、tomorrow）通常放在句尾，如 I will bring you the book tomorrow。

■ 地方副詞也常在句尾，但也可能位置稍前，因為要跟在動詞受詞或動詞之後，如果地方副詞和時間副詞同時出現，前者要在後者之前。

「Extra Bonus」

■ 簡單來説，如果句子比較短，時間副詞、地方副詞、及情態副詞經常都在句尾，長一點的句子就複雜一點，但不管怎樣，這些副詞都要在動詞或動詞的受詞之後。

「HOW」

■ 艾立克‧克萊普頓（Eric Clapton）在《天堂眼淚》（Tears in Heaven）這首歌中唱到：Would you know my name/If I saw you in heaven?/Would it be the same?/If I saw you in heaven.（如果我在天堂碰到你/你會知道我的名字嗎？/如果我在天堂碰到你/你會知道我的名字嗎？）

■ in heaven 是介系詞片語，作為副詞之用，這裡就是一個放在句尾的地方副詞，這樣的副詞片語就只能擺在句尾，功能在修飾動詞。如果說 You are in heaven. 此時 in heaven 就是作為主詞補語的形容詞片語。

「Extra Bonus」

■ 有些介系詞片語既可當形容詞，也可當副詞。如 in a hurry。

‧ There is no need to rush. I am not in a hurry. Come in a hurry.

「HOW」

■ 若以副詞所修飾的詞語來看,修飾動詞時,副詞通常位於主詞和動詞之間,或動詞和受詞之後。如 I often read books. 和 I read books carefully.修飾形容詞或副詞時,副詞通常放在所修飾的詞語之前。如 She gave him a really beautiful smile.和 We quite often go out to eat. 程度副詞通常用來修飾其他副詞,如 quite、almost、completely、extremely、rather、really、very 等。

■ 還有一種目的副詞,大多是不定詞片語,用來表達想要達成的目的,這類副詞也通常在句尾。

「Extra Bonus」

■ 表達目的的不定詞片語經常出現,只不過你可能不知道這些不定詞片語也是一種副詞。

· He got up early to catch the bus.

13-2 考試一點靈

文 法加油站

■ 前面提過如果地方副詞和時間副詞同時出現，把地方副詞放在時間副詞前面，但如果又有一個情態副詞該放哪裡？答案是擺在地方副詞前面。

· The girl sang the song happily in the bathroom yesterday evening.

■ 我們知道副詞要擺在助動詞和動詞之間，但如果有兩個副詞該怎麼擺？常見的是程度副詞和頻率副詞一起出現，此時程度副詞就要擺在頻率副詞前面做修飾。

· We can definitely never predict what will happen.

■ 助動詞通常放在 be 動詞之後，偶而也有出現在前面作為強調之用。

· I was never a fan of hers./I never was a fan of her.（強調從未）

實 戰句

❶ **Many migrant birds that breed in Europe spend the winter in Africa. A new satellite-tracking study shows that the wind conditions these birds encounter during their first migration-----determine where they go.**

(A) ever

(B) once

(C) largely

(D) rarely

中譯

　　許多在歐洲進行繁衍的候鳥冬季時飛到非洲大陸過冬，一份新的衛星追蹤研究顯示，這些鳥在第一次遷徙時所遭遇的風況大致決定了牠們要去哪裡。

考題最前端

　　這段文字有兩個句子。第一個句子是主詞+修飾主詞的形容詞子句+spend+受詞 winter+表示地方的副詞片語 in Africa。第二個句子是不定冠詞 a+形容詞 new satellite-tracking+主詞 study+動詞 shows+that 所引導的名詞子句，而 that 子句中的主詞是 wind conditions，主詞後面其實後面跟了一個形容詞子句，但由於關係代名詞（which 或 that）是受格可以省略，所以 that 子句中的動詞是 determine，前面空格裡顯然缺了一個副詞，largely 最符合上下文意。

答案：(C)

文 法加油站

■ 別忘了疑問副詞,疑問副詞是用來提出疑問的副詞,有 how、when、why、where 等。

　・How did he get the job?

■ 短副詞片語放在長副詞片語之前。

　・The old man takes a walk in a park before dawn almost every day.
　　(in a park 是地方副詞,按慣例放在時間副詞 before dawn 之前,而頻率副詞 almost every day 的時間較長)

■ 同類的副詞同時出現時,範圍較小的放在前面。

　・He lives in a small house in a suburban district.

實 戰句

❷ **In our imagination, dying is a lonely and meaningless process, but the final blog posts of -----ill patients and the last words of death row inmates are filled with love.**

(A) finally

(B) terminally

(C) constantly

(D) definitely

中譯

　在我們的想像中，死亡是一種既寂寞又毫無意義的過程，但晚期病人的最終部落格貼文和死刑犯的遺言卻充滿了愛。

考題最前端

　如果想要快一點答題，不想多花時間在分析句型上，可以直接看空格的前後，前面是介系詞 of，後面是 ill patients，顯然缺了一個修飾形容詞 ill 的副詞，這裡考的是一種慣用語，terminally ill patients 是指晚期病人，如果已經曉得這個慣用說法，就可以很快答出答案，如果沒有，稍微花點時間也猜得出來，因為其他三個答案套不進來。答案是 terminally。

答案：(B)

字詞辨析形容詞與副詞同形的字

單 元概述

形容詞與副詞同形的字有哪些？

有些字既可做形容詞也可做副詞，如 early、daily、hourly、weekly、quarterly、yearly、half、all、hard、easy、late、fast、slow、straight、just、clear、near、far、loud、low。以 weekly 為例，It is a weekly journal.=The journal comes out weekly.前一個是形容詞，後一個是副詞，weekly 還可做名詞，前面的例句也可說成 It is a weekly. 但不是每個表列的形容詞副詞同形的字都有這種三重用途。

14-1 文法修行 Let's Go

Q14 請問你都怎麼記憶形容詞副詞同形的字？有什麼更快的學習方式嗎？

「HOW」

■ 一般副詞以 ly 或 ily 結尾，但碰到形容詞副詞同形的字，這套規則就不管用，必須找出另一套記憶方法才行。這類字有幾類，像是時間的早晚（early、late）、頻率（daily、hourly、weekly 等）、事情的難易（hard、easy）、速度的快慢（fast、slow）、距離的遠近（far、near）、說話的輕重（loud、low）、事情或東西的比例（half、all、most）。這些分類幾乎涵蓋了大部分的形容詞副詞同形字。

「Extra Bonus」

■ 沒被列入分類的還有 straight、only、just、right 等，這些字比較難以歸入某一類別，卻很常出現，要特別注意。

　・She was right in her answer. /She guessed right. 前者為形容詞，後者為副詞。

「HOW」

■ 瑪丹娜（Madonna）在《數哩外》（Miles Away）這首歌中唱到：I just woke up from a fuzzy dream/You never would believe those things that I have seen/I looked in the mirror and I saw your face/You looked right through me, you were miles away（我從朦朧的夢中醒來/你永遠不會相信我見到了什麼/我看著鏡子看到你的臉/你看穿了我，你在數哩之外）。

■ You looked right through me.中的 right 就是副詞，意思是直接地、完全地、徹底地。I just woke up from a fuzzy dream.中的 just 也是副詞，意思是剛剛。

「Extra Bonus」

■ Miles away 的 away 看起來像是形容詞，其實是副詞。例如：The police station is two miles away.

· So, far, away 這三個字都是副詞，一個修飾一個，意思是那麼地遠。

「**HOW**」

■ 有些字具有兩種形式副詞，一是原形，另一是字尾加了 ly，如 close/closely、deep/deeply、direct/directly、fair/fairly、loud/loudly、quick/quickly、slow/slowly、wide/widely。這些字的副詞雖然有兩種形式，但意思大致是一樣，儘管有些微的不同。

■ 以 close/closely 為例，He held her close. 和 He held her closely. 這兩個句子都對，不過前者比較強調 He held her close to him. 也就是往他身體拉近的意思，而另一句的 closely 僅僅是在修飾動詞 held。再以 direct/directly 為例，I go directly to the airport. 和 I go direct to the airport. 都是正確的句子，不過第一句的 directly 是馬上的意思，而第二句的 direct 是直接的意思。

「**Extra Bonus**」

■ 這類例子雖不能算多，但偶而會碰到，還是要有一定的認識才行。再以 fair/fairly 為例。

· 我們說 play fair 和 fight fair 時，通常都會用 fair 來代替 fairly，意思就是公平地競賽。

14-2 考試一點靈

文 法加油站

■ 有些動詞就是慣用字尾沒有 ly 的副詞，如 go slow、drive slow、run slow、come close、open your mouth wide。

- My watch runs slow.

■ 有些字有兩種形式和意義都不同的副詞，如 hard/hardly、free/freely、high/highly、late/lately、pretty/prettily。

- He works so hard that he hardly has time to spend with his family.

■ 有幾個經常讓人搞不清楚的表達方式，如 fold it tight 和 fold it tightly，兩種表達方式都對，但意義上有些微的差異，tight 表達狀態，tightly 強調 fold 的動作。

- Good night, sleep tight.

實 戰句

❶ **New research findings show that eating late at night poses a greater risk to health than commonly thought. Time-delayed eating, as compared to eating earlier in the day, can increase weight, insulin and cholesterol levels, and-----affect fat metabolism.**

(A) positively

(B) negatively

(C) very

(D) far

中譯

　　新的研究發現顯示，晚上吃得晚對健康造成的危害大於一般所想的。與較早用餐相比，晚吃會增加體重、胰島素和膽固醇，對脂肪代謝有負面的影響。

考題最前端

　　熟悉文法句型的同學很快就可看出空格裡缺一個修飾動詞 affect 的副詞，由於產生的是負面影響，必須選 negatively。這裡比較會讓人產生困惑是兩個 and，第一個 and 連接 increase 的三個受詞，三個受詞中的第一個和第二個間用逗號分開，第二個和第三個間用 and 連接。第二個 and 則是連接兩個動詞，亦即 increase 和 affect。搞清楚關係後，答案就呼之欲出。

答案：(B)

文 法加油站

■ Half 這個字通常用作名詞或形容詞，其實作副詞的機會也不少。

· She was half crying, half laughing.

■ Most 也是當形容詞和代名詞的機會較多，但和最高級一起用時一定是副詞。

· This is the most expensive watch I have bought.

■ Good 和 well 意義相近，可是前者是形容詞，後者是副詞。

· She plays the piano well.（不可用 good 代替 well）

實 戰句

❷ **There is no affectation about true feelings, and as they come-----from your heart, so they go straight to mine. A heart that values true feelings understands what it takes to be loved.**

(A) slowly

(B) slow

(C) straight

(D) straightly

中譯

真實的感情沒有作假，正如它直接來自妳的心，它也直接進入我的心。珍惜感情的心懂得要怎樣才能被愛。

考題最前端

這題用到一個特殊的句型（just）as... so...，意思是正如...，也...。舉例來說：Just as French people enjoy their wine, so the Chinese enjoy their tea.這個句型把兩件事情拿來相比擬。懂得這個句型後就知道 as 和 so 後面都跟著一個獨立的子句，各有自己的主詞和動詞，come 和 from your heart 之間顯然缺一個副詞，straight 最符合上下文意。

答案：(C)

認識代名詞

單 元概述

何謂代名詞？有何功用？

顧名思義，代名詞是用來代替名詞或名詞片語的字詞，其功用是避免讓同一個名詞反覆出現，讓句子變得單調乏味。被代替的名詞或名詞片語稱為先行詞。代名詞真的是用來避免重複，但有些同學或許會問，難道一直重複同一名詞不行嗎？理論上可以，但實際上很少人這麼做，因為會讓句子看起來很累贅。譬如，The police are respected by most people because the police maintain social security and traffic order. 第二次提到 police 時，最好用代名詞 they 來代替。

15-1 文法修行 Let's Go

Q15 請問你都怎麼記憶代名詞？有什麼更快的學習方式嗎？

「HOW」

■ 代名詞很多，最常見的是我、你、他（或她）這類人稱代名詞，英文分別是 I, you, he or she，這些是單數的主格代名詞，它們還有受格代名詞，即 me, you, him or her。如果是複數，主格為 we, you, they，受格為 us, you, them。對初學者來說，實在有點不太好記。可以想一些口訣來增加記憶，像是用「艾咪威厄斯」來表示第一人稱代名詞從單數主受格到複數主受格的變化，也就是 I, me, we, us。第二人稱 you 最簡單，不管主格受格或單數複數，形式都是一樣。

「Extra Bonus」

■ 第三人稱的人稱代名詞比較複雜，因為要分男性和女性，男性的 he, him, they, them 和女性的 she, her, they, them，它們在單數時有些不同，複數時則完全一樣。

■ 世界知名皇后搖滾樂團（Queen）有一首膾炙人口的歌曲，叫做〈我們要讓你搖滾起來〉（We Will Rock You）。裡面反覆出現 We will rock you. 這個句子，我想大家都能朗朗上口。

■ 句子裡的 you 就是第二人稱的受格代名詞，可以是單數，也可以是複數，但歌曲是對著一群人在唱，所以應該是複數。皇后樂團還有另一首無人不知無人不曉的歌曲，叫做〈我們是冠軍〉（We Are the Champions），如果想不起來，只要聽到旋律就能馬上恢復記憶。

「Extra Bonus」

■ 兩首歌曲的歌名用到了兩個代名詞，即 we 和 you。We 是兩首歌名的主詞，為複數的第一人稱主格代名詞。We are the champions.也可以說成 You are the champions. 但意義就變成「你們是冠軍」，而不是「我們是冠軍」。

「HOW」

■ 飲食中有糖和代糖，本來代糖只是代用品，但也可以獨立出來組成某種食品的糖味。同樣地，代名詞本來是用來代替名詞，但也可以單獨使用，不一定要代替某個名詞。

■ 在對話時，由於知道誰是誰，就直接用人稱代名詞來代替我、你、他（或她）。代名詞中有不定代名詞，像是 everybody, anybody, something, everything，這類代名詞通常可以獨立使用，因為沒有明顯地代替任何名詞，只是泛指任何一人或事物。

「Extra Bonus」

■ 不定代名詞很常出現，以 one 為例，由於沒有特別指任何一人，所以可以用來描述一般性事情，例如，One cannot master a language unless he tries very hard to learn it.

15-2 考試一點靈

文 法加油站

■ 主格代名詞可以作為一個句子的開始，如之前幾個例子所示。

· We are the champions, not the losers.

■ 主格代名詞可以放在主詞補語的位置，尤其是在 It is…that…這種分裂句中。

· It was she that/who made the decision.

■ 不定代名詞沒有先行詞，可以獨立使用。

· No one likes the smell of stinky tofu.

實 戰句

❶ Rising temperatures caused by global warming will make-----harder for aircraft around the world to take off in the future. Around 10 to 30 percent of planes fully loaded with passengers may have to remove some fuel or wait for cooler hours to fly.

(A) them

(B) its

(C) it

(D) they

中譯

　　全球暖化所引起的氣溫上升未來將使世界各地的飛機越來越難降落。約 10%至 30%的滿載乘客飛機可能要減少油料或等氣溫較涼爽時才能起飛。

考題最前端

　　這一題在考 it 這個代名詞的用法。It 通常用來代替事物，也可指人。它可作為虛主詞或虛受詞。It is important for a student to study hard.和 It cost me NT$250 to buy the ticket.這兩個句子就是標準的以 it 作為虛主詞的例子，真正的主詞是後面的不定詞片語 to study hard 和 to buy the ticket。作為虛受詞，it 會出現在 make 這類使役動詞後面，後面再跟著不定詞片語，例如，He makes it a rule to take a walk every day.受詞後面還有受詞補語，名詞或形容詞皆可，所以答案是 C。

答案：(C)

■ 受格代名詞可以作為直接受詞、間接受詞、介系詞受詞。它們包括 me, you, him, her, them, us, it。

・ The teacher talked to her about the mistake.

■ except 這類介系詞後面要接受格代名詞,很多人經常搞錯,還是用主格代名詞。

・ No one in our class knows how to play golf except you and me.

■ 不管是主格還是受格,人稱代名詞的順序總是把 I 或 me 放在後面。

・ My friend and I plan to go swimming.

實 戰句

❷ **Many people who have had a near-death experience have a lot to say about what-----experienced while being close to death or impending death. Such experiences can take many different shapes. Some of the well-known experiences include having an out-of-body experience and perceiving a tunnel.**

(A) we

(B) you

(C) it

(D) they

中譯

　　許多有過瀕死經驗的人對他們接近死亡那一刻的體驗都有許多的東西可以說。這類經驗以許多不同形式出現，一些著名的經驗包括靈魂出竅和看見一條隧道。

考題最前端

　　在這段文字的第一個句子裡，主詞是 many people，後面 who 引導的形容詞子句在修飾主詞，動詞為 have，a lot 為其受詞，後面接不定詞，介系詞 about 後面接一由疑問代名詞 what 所引導的名詞子句，在這個子句中，空格之後出現動詞 experienced，顯然缺的是一個主詞，而這個主詞指的就是前面提到的 many people，此時要用 they 來代替。答案是 D。

答案：(D)

認識關係代名詞

單 元概述

何謂關係代名詞？有何功用？

關係代名詞引導一個附屬子句並代替前面所提到的名詞或代名詞（先行詞），兼具代名詞和連接詞的功能，既然是代名詞的一種，也就具有主格、受格、及所有格形式。這些關係代名詞有 who、whom、which、that、whose、what、whomever、whoever 等，最常出現的是前五種。

16-1 文法修行 Let's Go

Q16 請問你都怎麼關係代名詞？有什麼更快的學習方式嗎？

「HOW」

■ 關係代名詞是一種表明關係的代名詞，一方面代替先行詞，一方面連接兩個句子，既然表明關係，就要越近越好，所以通常關係代名詞引導的子句緊接著在先行詞之後出現。

■ 關係代名詞中又以 that 最好用，也最常出現，因為它除了指人，還可指物，所以可以代替 who、whom、which，也就是既能當主格，也能當受格，當然有些例外的狀況，但基本上用途最為廣泛。

「Extra Bonus」

■ 不能使用 that 的狀況主要有二，一是介系詞之後，二是非限定附屬子句。換言之，就是不能在介系詞後面用 that，也不能在非限定附屬子句後面用，所謂的非限定附屬子句，就是前有逗號的那種，沒有逗號的叫做限定。

「HOW」

■ 加拿大女歌手夏妮雅・特恩（Shania Twain）在她的知名歌曲〈你還是我屬意的那個人〉（You're Still The One）中用到不少關係代名詞：You're still the one I run to; /The one that I belong to. /You're still the one I want for life.（你還是我奔向的那個人/那個我屬於的人/你還是那個我想要終生擁有的人）。

■ You're still the one I run to.這個句子省略了受格代名詞 whom 或 that，原來應該是 You're still the one whom/that I run to.下一個句子就保留了關係代名詞 that：the one that I belong to。

「Extra Bonus」

■ 同學們或許會有疑問，不是說 that 不能和介系詞一起用嗎？別搞錯了，是不能在介系詞後面接 that，如果介系詞在 that 的後面就沒問題了。例如，You're still the one to whom I belong. 把介系詞 to 放到關係代名詞前面，此時就不能用 that 來代替。

「HOW」

■ 有關係代名詞的句子最常出現的問題是什麼時候要用逗號分開關係代名詞所連接的兩個句子，能把這個問題搞懂，就能事半功倍。

■ 只要用到逗號，後面的關係代名詞就不能用 that，只能用 who 或 whom，而什麼時候用逗號，就要看是否為非限定附屬子句。非限定附屬子句要用逗號和前面的主要子句分開，而限定附屬子句則不需要逗號，此時就能和 that 做替換。

「Extra Bonus」

■ 所謂限定附屬子句就是特定指某個人，例如，I don't know the woman who is smiling at me.而非限定就是不用特別指出他人就能明白，例如，More and more foreign tourists visit Taipei, which is attractive in its own way.

16-2 考試一點靈

文 法加油站

■ who 只能指人，通常作主詞，也可以作為受格，此時能和 whom 相互替換。

  · This is George, who/whom you met just yesterday.

■ whom 只能指人，且只能作受詞，如果 whom 前面有介系詞，不能用 who 或 that 來替代。

  · He is the one to whom she runs to./He is the one whom/who/that she runs to.

■ which 只能指物，可以作主詞和受詞。

  · We bought a tool, with which we finished the job.

實 戰句

❶ A recent development in the energy industry has been to replace unsafe and expensive lithium-ion batteries with zinc-anode versions out of cost and safety concerns. For the moment, the only disadvantage of this new battery has been its relatively short cycle life,----- has not allowed it to be successfully commercialized.

(A) which

(B) who

(C) whom

(D) that

中譯

　　能源產業最近的一項發展是把不安全且昂貴鋰離子電池用鋅陽極電池加以替換，原因是出於成本和安全考量。目前這種電池的唯一缺點是生命週期太短，以致於無法使其成功地商業化。

考題最前端

　　這個題目要考的顯然不是牽涉到人的關係代名詞，因為從頭到尾都在講電池，可以先排除 who 和 whom 作為答案的可能性，接下來剩下 which 和 that，問題是 that 不能放在逗號之後，最後只有 which 符合文法需求。which 除了指物外，還可以涵蓋前面主要子句所代表的意義，這裡指的就是新電池生命週期太短一事。答案是 A。

答案：(A)

■ 有時候關係代名詞要和介系詞一起連用才能使意思完整，此時介系詞有兩個擺法，一是在關係代名詞前面，另一是在關係代名詞所引導的子句最後面。

- This is the house which we live in. /This is the house in which we live./This is the house we live in.

■ 關係代名詞和人稱代名詞不能同時並用，也就是說，當關係代名詞代替了前面的先行詞後，它所引導的子句就不能再用人稱代名詞來指稱先行詞。

She is the woman whom Peter wants. 是正確的句子，而 She is the woman whom Peter wants her.就是錯誤的句子。

■ 關係代名詞除了 who, which, that, what 外，還有所謂複合關係代名詞，這些包括 whoever, whomever, whichever, whatever, whosesoever 等。這類關係代名詞還有連接詞的功能，可以獨立引導出一個附屬子句。

- Whoever comes to the door, tell them I am not at home.

實 戰句

❷ **The percentage of fatally injured drivers-----tested positive for prescription opioids rose from 1 percent in 1995 to over 7 percent in 2015, according to a new study**

by a medical school in the U.S. Of drivers testing positive for prescription opioids, 30 percent also had higher blood alcohol concentrations.

(A) which

(B) whom

(C) whose

(D) who

中譯

在因車禍受到致命傷害的駕駛當中,對處方用類鴉片藥物測試呈現陽性反應的人數比例,已從 1995 年的 1%上升到 2015 年的 7%,這是根據美國一所醫學院最新的研究報告。在這些對類鴉片藥物測試呈現陽性反應的駕駛當中,30%的血液裡也有較高的酒精濃度。

考題最前端

這題是在測試同學對主格關係代名詞的熟悉度,空格裡缺的顯然是和人有關的關係代名詞,由於後面有動詞 tested,所以可以確認是 who。The percentage of fatally injured drivers testing positive for prescription opioids rose….這個句子可以改成 The percentage of fatally injured drivers testing positive for prescription opioids rose…重點在於把 who 去掉後,動詞改成分詞形式,其他部分保持原狀即可。

答案:(D)

認識指示代名詞

單 元概述

何謂指示代名詞？有何功用？

指示代名詞是用來指出句子中特定的人、物或詞語，可以表示時間和距離上的遠近。這些代名詞包括 this, these, that, those，當後面有名詞時，還可以作為形容詞用，有人稱其為指示形容詞，但不管是哪種，形式都是一樣，還是 this, these, that, those。

17-1 文法修行 Let's Go

Q17 請問你都怎麼記憶指示代名詞？有什麼更快的學習方式嗎？

「HOW」

■ 簡單來說，我們可以用時間和距離上的遠近來判斷什麼時候用 this, these，什麼時候用 that, those。近的事物當然用 this, these，遠的事物則用 that, those。如何判斷遠近，就要看上下文而定。

■ 譬如說，幫我拿桌上的那本書，英文是 Bring me that book from the table. 既然請人幫忙拿，顯然離自己有段距離，所以只能說 that book，不可能說 this book，因為邏輯上不通。不過對某些懶人來說，不管距離多遠，就算只有一步之遙，也會找人幫忙。

「Extra Bonus」

■ 講電話時最常用到 this 和 that。譬如，Hello. This is Paul. Is that Peter?

■ 皇后樂團有一首歌廣泛地用到指示代名詞 these 和 those，這首歌叫做〈這些是我們生命中的日子〉（These Are the Days of Our Lives）。歌詞中有這一段：Those were the days of our lives/The bad things in life were so few/Those days are all gone now.（那些是我們生命中的日子/生命中的壞事是那麼地少/那些日子現在都已不見。）

■ 由於是講過去的日子，所以用 those 來表示，不過歌曲的曲名卻用 These are the days of our lives. 而不是歌詞裡的 Those are the days of our lives. 合理的解釋是創作者在回憶的同時，也把過去的時光帶到當下。正常的狀況下還是要用 those 來表示比較遙遠的過去。

「Extra Bonus」

■ 英國文豪莎士比亞的劇作《暴風雨》（The Tempest）中有一名句：Those were the pearls that were his eyes.

144

「HOW」

■ 補充說明 this 和 that 的區別。當你在介紹兩個人時，距離你比較近的那個，你會說 This is Sally. 距離你比較遠的那個，你就說 That is Nick.其實這兩人距離都差不多，只不過以你的角度來看，Sally 比較近，而 Nick 比較遠。

■ 再舉一個例子，當有人送禮物給你時，你拿在手上尚未拆開禮物，此時可以問，What is this? 此時你的眼睛瞄到對方還有另一件禮物要送你，可是還沒拿給你，也沒說要送你，你只能問，What is that? 因為東西還不是你的，所以用 that。

「Extra Bonus」

■ 英語有一個片語，叫做 this and that，意思是各種各樣的事情。

  · "What were you talking about" "Oh, this and that."

17-2 考試一點靈

文 法加油站

■ this 和 that 可以用來指出已經出現過的子句或句子內容。

· He said he had finished his homework, but that was a lie.

■ 指示代名詞作主詞時，可以指人和物，但作受詞時只能指物。

· This is my friend Ted.

■ that 和 those 可以用來避免重複已經提過的名詞。

· Taiwan has a land area much smaller than that of China.

實 戰句

❶ It seems that any behavior can be "gamified" and awarded digital points these days, from tracking your walking steps to your online purchases. Tracking behavior in-----way helps to spur further action. New research shows that even meaningless scores can serve as effective motivators.

(A) these

(B) this

(C) the

(D) same

中譯

　　近來似乎任何行為都可以被「遊戲化」並賦予數位分數，從你的步行數到線上採購皆可。這樣的追蹤行為有助於刺激更進一步行動。新的研究顯示即使是毫無意義的分數也能作為有效的促動因素。

考題最前端

　　前面提過 this 和 that 可以代替同一文章已經提過的概念或詞語，這一題就是在測驗同學的理解程度。tracking 是作為主詞的動名詞，behavior 是其受詞，in this way 是作為副詞的介系詞片語，修飾tracking，動詞是 helps。把 this 改成 that 是否可以? 文法上應該沒錯，但 this 表示所提的是同一件事，用 that 則有從現在討論的事情抽離出來的味道，所以還是用 this 比較好。

答案：(B)

文 法加油站

■ this/these 可以指正在發生或即將開始的狀況和經驗。

- Listen to this. You'll like it.

■ that/those 可以指剛結束或很久以前的經驗。

- Did you see that?

■ that 可以用來指某件事情的結束。

- And that's how it happened.

實 戰句

❷ **The researchers next wanted to find out whether-----progressive loss of stem cells was actually causing aging and was not just associated with it. So they observed what happened when they selectively disrupted the hypothalamic stem cells in middle-aged mice.**

(A) this

(B) those

(C) same

(D) it

中譯

　　研究人員接著想要發現這種漸進式的幹細胞流失是否實際導致了老化，而不是只有關聯性而已。所以他們選擇性地擾亂中年老鼠的下視丘幹細胞，進而發現是怎麼一回事。

考題最前端

　　如果是正在討論或關切的議題通常用 this 來代替，用 that 就有離開這一議題的意味，所以如果前後探討的是一個連貫的議題，用 this 就沒錯了。這一題一開始雖然沒有說 this progressive loss of stem cells 是怎麼一回事，但出題者不會讓考生陷入一種毫無頭緒的猜測之中，碰到這種情況，考生應該可以放心地認定是在講一個前後連貫的議題，所以答案是A。

答案：(A)

了解現在分詞和過去分詞的差異

單 元概述

何謂現在分詞和過去分詞？有何功用？

現在分詞和過去分詞是動詞的兩種分詞形式，現在分詞以 ing 為結尾，過去分詞大多以 ed 為結尾，也有很多以 en 為結尾。現在分詞搭配 be 動詞構成進行式，而過去分詞搭配助動詞 have 構成完成式或與 be 動詞形成被動式。現在分詞和過去分詞都可以作為形容詞或副詞，但前者有主動或正在進行的意思，後者有被動或已經完成的意思。

18-1 文法修行 Let's Go

Q18 請問你都怎麼記憶現在分詞和過去分詞？有什麼更快的學習方式嗎？

「HOW」

■ 其實也沒那麼難，以 interest 這個動詞為例，現在分詞是 interesting，過去分詞是 interested。interest 的現在分詞純粹用作形容詞，無法搭配 be 動詞構成現在進行式，也就是沒有正在感興趣這種說法。interest 的過去分詞和 be 動詞搭配也不是在表示被什麼東西吸引，而是對什麼東西感興趣。舉例來說，The book interests me. /I am interested in the book. /The book is interesting to me. 這三個句子的意思都一樣，只是用過去分詞和現在分詞有不同的表達方式。

「Extra Bonus」

■ 類似的例子很多，如 boring/bored, exciting/excited, surprising/surprised 等。

· The movie was boring to me./I was bored by the movie.

Part I 基礎實力養成篇

Part II 進階文法修練篇

「**HOW**」

■ 美國旅行者（Journey）搖滾樂團在〈不要停止相信〉（Don't Stop Believing）這首歌中唱到：Just a small-town girl/Livin' in a lonely world/ She took the midnight train/Goin' anywhere（只是一個小鎮女孩/活在一個寂寞的世界裡/她搭上午夜火車/四處去旅行）。

■ living 是 live 的現在分詞，living in a lonely world 為一修飾 girl 的分詞片語，原來的句型是形容詞子句 who lived in a lonely world，只要把主格關係代名詞 who 去掉，動詞改為分詞形式即可。

「**Extra Bonus**」

■ 被動形式的關係代名詞子句也可以改成分詞片語。

- a small-town girl who is not interested in city life/a small-town girl not interested in city life

「HOW」

■ 現在分詞作為形容詞時通常是指對某人產生情緒上的作用，像是 exciting, interesting, boring, surprising, troubling，通常接介系詞 to，再接人。例如，The movie is exciting/interesting/boring to me.或 The result was surprising/troubling to me. 這些分詞形容詞的特點都是擺在主詞補語的位置。

■ 相較之下，過去分詞作為形容詞則有比較多的規則，尤其是後面所接的介系詞，像是 be interested in, be excited about, be surprised at, be tired of，be confused about 它們所接的介系詞五花八門，一不小心就容易弄錯。要記住，這些過去分詞形容詞都要以人為主詞，而不是物。Something is interesting.才對，Something is interested.則是錯的。

「Extra Bonus」

■ 現在分詞形容詞通常可以作為敘述形容詞（放在主詞補語位置）和限定形容詞（放在名詞之前），而過去分詞形容詞通常作為敘述形容詞之用。

・The book is interesting. /It is an interesting book.不能説 It is an interested book.

18-2 考試一點靈

文 法加油站

■ 少數不及物動詞的過去分詞也能修飾名詞，但為數不多，修飾名詞的還是以現在分詞為主。

  · a fallen leave（落葉），a falling leave（飄在空中的葉子）

■ 及物動詞的過去分詞被用來修飾名詞的例子不少，尤其是在飲食領域。

  · fried chicken，boiled egg，iced tea

■ 辨別分詞形容詞是否為正確，試著改成關係子句看看，如果能通，就對了。

  · running water/water that runs，singing brook/brook that sings，shaking knee/knee that shakes，fried chicken/chicken that has been fried，boiled egg/egg that has been boiled，developed countries/countries that have developed，developing countries/countries that are developing

實 戰句

❶ **Researchers have examined how people react to robots-----faulty behavior compared to those working without a**

glitch. It turns out that people participating in the probe took a significantly stronger fondness for the faulty robot than the robot interacting flawlessly.

(A) exhibited

(B) exhibit

(C) exhibiting

(D) have exhibited

中譯

研究人員調查人們對行為出錯的機器人有何反應,與之對比的是表現完美的機器人。結果顯示參與調查的人顯著地對出錯的機器人,而非互動無誤的機器人,有著比較強烈的喜好。

考題最前端

這段文字中出現很多現在分詞,像是 working 和 interacting。有一個方法可以確認分詞,就是改成關係子句。例如,those working without a glitch 可以改成 those that work without a glitch,robots interacting flawlessly 可以改成 robots that interact flawlessly。如果通順就沒錯了。robots exhibiting faulty behavior 改成 robots that exhibit faulty behavior 也沒問題,所以答案是 C。

答案:(C)

文 法加油站

■ 現在複合形容詞越來越流行，其形式是副詞+連字號+過去分詞。

- a recently-built house，a newly-developed product，a hard-won battle

■ 複合形容詞也有另一種形式，即形容詞+分詞。

- a good-looking person，a middle-aged woman

■ 要確定這些複合形容詞是否無誤，也可以改成關係子句看看，如果通順就對了。

- a recently-built house/a house that has recently been built，a newly-developed product/a product that has newly been developed，a good-looking person/a person that looks good.

實 戰句

❷ **Researchers are-----to insects -- specifically cicadas -- for understanding of the design of artificial surfaces capable of de-icing and self-cleaning. Cicadas are also good at repelling water. It is assumed that wetland-dwelling cicadas have the most water-repellant wings.**

(A) look

(B) looked

(C) looking

(D) have looked

中譯

　　研究人員現在轉向昆蟲－－特別是蟬－－尋求了解要如何設計出具有除冰、自我清潔能力的人造表面。蟬也善於防水，居住在濕地的蟬被認定為擁有最具防水能力的翅膀。

考題最前端

　　Be 動詞搭配現在分詞構成現在進行式，這題一開始就透露這樣的結構，很顯然是 look 的現在分詞 looking。de-icing 和 self-cleaning 則是動名詞，作為 of 的受詞。wetland-dwelling 則是複合形容詞的一種，wetland-dwelling cicadas 就是 cicadas that dwell in wetland。water-repellant 也是一種複合形容詞，但不在我們討論的範圍。

答案：(C)

It feels like 和
I feel like 的差異

單 元概述

何謂 *It feels like* 和 *I feel like*？有何區別？

常常有人把這兩種說法搞混，其實它們的意思大為不同，前者是似乎、好像的意思，後者則是感覺像是或想要做某件事的意思。有人說，*It feels like drinking coffee*，意思是感覺像在喝咖啡，如果想要表達的是我想要喝咖啡，則要說 *I feel like drinking coffee.*

19-1 文法修行 Let's Go

Q19 請問你都怎麼理解 It feels like 和 I feel like？有什麼更快的學習方式嗎？

「HOW」

■ 日常生活比較常用的是 I feel like，雖然它和 It feels like 基本上是不同的概念。舉例來說，我覺得像是個傻子，英文是 I feel like a fool. 而不是 It feels like a fool. 先把 I feel like 的用法和意思搞懂，就不會和 It feels like 搞混。

■ I feel like 的另一個意思是想要做某件事，後面要接動名詞。我想要離開的英文是 I feel like leaving. 有人可能會寫成 I feel like to leave. 這是不對的，因為 like 在這裡不是動詞，而是介系詞。

「Extra Bonus」

■ 和 I feel like 有關的慣用語有 feel like oneself，意思是覺得身體狀況正常。

· She asked for a leave today because she didn't feel like herself.

「HOW」

■ 美國搖滾樂團班克斯（Banks）在〈感覺就是這樣〉（This Is What It Feels Like）這首歌曲中唱到：I see you trying to pretend/Like I'm making it up/This is what it feels like（我看到你嘗試假裝/好像我在編造一般/感覺就是這樣）

■ 這裡的 what it feels like 比較像是 I feel like，美式英文在口語上有點把這兩種說法混在一起，也可以用 it feels like 來代替 I feel like，但在正規的書寫英文中，這兩種說法還是有所不同。

「Extra Bonus」

■ 雖然在口語用法上有相互替換的趨勢，但有些狀況還是不能適用。

・I feel like having ice cream. 不能用 It feels like having ice cream. 來代替。

「**HOW**」

■ I feel like 通常後面接名詞或動名詞，不會接一個句子，但口語上越來越多人在後面接一個句子，像是 I feel like I am dying. 很常聽人說到這個句子，更怪的是，也有人說 It feels like I am dying.

這是怎麼一回事？

■ I feel like I am dying. 是描述切身的感受，感覺像是要死了一般，而 It feels like I am dying. 則是抽離出來，表示那種感覺好像快死了一般，雖然也很強烈，但不如 I feel like I am dying. 來得直接。

「**Extra Bonus**」

■ 類似 It feels like+句子的句型還有 It looks like

　· It looks like it might rain.

19-2 考試一點靈

文 法加油站

■ 在書寫上，如果一定要在 It feels like 後面接一個句子，最好改成 It feels as if，這樣就沒問題了。

· It feels as if I have been cheated.

■ 口語上可以在 I feel like 後接一個句子，但正式的書寫文章中不能這麼用。

· 不要說 I feel like I am an idiot. 直接說 I feel like an idiot.就可以，此舉能避免畫蛇添足。

■ 在書寫文章中如果要在 I feel like 後面接一個句子，要改成 I feel as if 或 I feel as though，才是正確的文法。

· 不要說 I feel like I saw you before. 要說 I feel like as if（as though）I saw you before.

實 戰句

❶ **What does-----feel like to bring a Mediterranean diet to your table? Mediterranean diets have been linked to a reduction in cardiovascular risk. However, the health benefits are observed only in people with higher**

educational level or greater household income. The less advantaged groups don't seem to get any actual benefits.

(A) he

(B) it

(C) they

(D) she

中譯

　　採用地中海膳食是一種怎樣的感覺？地中海膳食與心血管風險的降低有關聯，然而，這些健康上的好處只有在教育程度比較高或家庭收入比較高的人的身上看到，條件沒那麼好的人似乎沒有得到實質的好處。

考題最前端

　　也可以用 What does it feel like…?來問問題，記住後面要接不定詞片語，完整的句子是 What does it feel like to bring a Mediterranean diet to your table?這樣問通常是問一些自己沒有親身經歷或只能靠想像的事情，像是 What does it feel like to die? 沒有人可以回答這個問題，因為人死了就死了，沒辦法告訴別人是怎樣的感覺，當然也有少數死而復生的例子，但那是例外，而不是通例。

答案：(B)

■ feel 後面接 as if 和 as though 是在表達一種感覺，如果是 feel that，則意思完全不同，是在陳述一種看法。

· I feel that she will make a good wife.

■ It feels as if+句子通常被用來隱匿地表達主觀的看法，比直接用 I feel as if 好，感覺比較客觀。

· It feels as if the government is ready to compromise with the protestors.

■ It feels+形容詞+不定詞片語也是一種用看似客觀的方式來表達主觀感受的句型。

· It feels good to have a situation like that.

實 戰句

❷ **Existing studies have indicated that physical punishment, such as spanking, has negative impact on child development. Many people experiencing trauma during childhood-----disconnected and withdrawn as they transition into adulthood. Now a new study has found that physical discipline experienced during infancy can negatively impact behavior among children.**

(A) feeling

(B) feel

(C) fallen

(D) to feel

中譯

　　現有的研究顯示，打屁股之類的體罰對孩子的成長有負面的影響。許多孩童時期經歷過創傷的人在步入成年時會感到孤立與退縮。現在一項新的研究發現，幼年時期所受的體罰會對孩童造成負面的影響。

考題最前端

　　這題很簡單，就在考你對句型的分析能力。Many people experiencing trauma during childhood 是句子的主詞和修飾主詞的分詞片語，本來應該是 Many people who experience trauma during childhood，這種主格關係代名詞所引導的子句可以改成分詞片語，把 who 去掉，動詞改成現在分詞即可。feel disconnected and withdrawn 是句子的動詞和主詞補語，而 as they transition into adulthood 則是由 as 所引導的子句。所以答案是 B。

答案：(B)

了解動名詞 Ving 的意義

單 元概述

何謂動名詞？有何功用？

動名詞和現在分詞在形態上一樣，都是字尾加 ing，可是前者基本上是具有動詞型態的名詞，可以作為主詞、主詞補語、受詞、及介系詞的受詞，但本身也可以接受詞或有副詞修飾，就這一點而言，還保有動詞的特性。而現在分詞基本上除了和 be 動詞構成進行式外，主要的功能是作為形容詞。

20-1 文法修行 Let's Go

Q20 請問你都怎麼記憶動名詞？有什麼更快的學習方式嗎？

「HOW」

■ 我們很常看到動名詞，只是沒特別去分這是動名詞還是分詞。像是路邊或室內的禁制標誌 No Parking、No Cycling、No Smoking，這些不難理解，但如何在句子中區別哪些是動名詞哪些是現在分詞就比較難了。

■ 舉個最簡單的例子，I like eating.這裡的 eating 是動名詞，作為動詞 like 的受詞，也可以說 I like food. 但就沒像動名詞 eating 那樣具有動作的意味。也可以說 Eating is what I like. 此時 eating 就是主詞，What I like is eating. 也說得通，此時是主詞補語。

「Extra Bonus」

■ be 動詞加上 ing 也可以作為動名詞，很多人會在這個地方搞錯。

· I don't like being a politician.

「HOW」

■ 愛爾蘭樂團西城男孩（Westlife）在〈曼蒂〉（Mandy）這首歌中唱到：Well you came and you gave without taking /But I sent you away, oh Mandy/Well you kissed me and stopped me from shaking（妳來了後只給予不拿取/我卻要妳走，噢，曼蒂/妳親了我讓我不再顫抖）裡面的 taking 和 shaking 都是動名詞，作為介系詞 without 和 from 的受詞，本質上是名詞。

■ stop... from 這類片語動詞要靠記憶，不同的動詞搭配不同的介系詞構成不同的片語動詞，這只能靠記憶，沒有明顯的捷徑可言。

「Extra Bonus」

■ 我們常用 How about V-ing?表示去做…如何？

・How about going out for a walk?

「**HOW**」

■ 有些動詞後面只能接動名詞，像是 enjoy, finish, quit, feel like, avoid, consider, deny, give up, keep, mind, resist。有些動詞後面可以接不定詞，也可以接動名詞，意思完全一樣，像是 start, begin, continue, like, hate，這些動詞比較會人產生疑惑，以為後面接動名詞或不定詞的意義不一樣，事實上沒有任何的不同，只是習慣哪一種的問題。

■ 但如果碰上被動語態的動名詞，可能會比較複雜一點。例如，I don't like being watched. 和 I don't like to be watched. 都可以，不要被稍微複雜一點的結構給嚇到了。

「**Extra Bonus**」

■ 有些動詞後面只能接不定詞，像是 plan, ask, decide, learn, intend。

・He plans to study abroad.

20-2 考試一點靈

文 法加油站

■ 動名詞當主詞時通常放在句首。

  · Reading books is a good habit.

■ 偶而也出現作為主詞的動名詞放在句尾，此時要用到 it 作為虛主詞，這樣的句型類似以不定詞作為主詞的句型。

  · It is enjoyable doing nothing at all.

■ 動名詞擺在 be 動詞後作為主詞補語時，容易讓人誤以為是進行式。

  · My hobby is reading books.

實 戰句

❶ Since-----the social media platform Twitter in 2009, Trump has issued more than 35,000 messages. This amounts to about twelve tweets a day. With 30 million followers, he is the second most followed politician on Twitter after his predecessor, Barack Obama, who on average tweeted about four times a day.

(A) joining

(B) join

(C) joined

(D) have joined

中譯

　　自從 2009 年加入社群媒體平台推特後，川普總共發了 3 萬 5000 則推文，相當於一天約 12 則推文。擁有 3000 萬追隨者的他，是推特上追隨人數第二高的政客，僅次於前任總統歐巴馬，歐巴馬平均一天發 4 則推文。

考題最前端

　　這題主要測驗考生對 since 用法的熟悉度。since 可以作為連結詞和介系詞，作連接詞時表示原因和時間，後面接一個附屬子句。作介系詞時表示時間，後面接動名詞。since 所引導的附屬子句可以改為以介系詞 since 所引導的片語，只要把主詞去掉，動詞改成 V-ing 即可。Since he joined the social media platform Twitter in 2009, Trump has issued….可以改成 Since joining the social media platform Twitter in 2009, Trump has issued….。所以答案是 A。

答案：(A)

文 法加油站

■ 動名詞有其意義上的主詞,若是和實際的主詞一致時維持原樣,不用加任何字詞。

  · Mr. Wang doesn't like riding his bicycle.

■ 當動名詞意義上的主詞和實際的主詞不一致時,必須用所有格或受格代名詞來表出意義上的主詞。

  · My brother doesn't like my riding his bicycle.

■ 動名詞的否定形式是在動名詞之前放 not 或 never。

  · Not coming on time is rude.

實 戰句

❶ Up to 75 percent of patients with systemic lupus erythematosus experience neuropsychiatric symptoms. But so far, our-----of the mechanisms underlying lupus' effects on the brain has remained cloudy. There is still a long way to find a real cure.

(A) understand

(B) understood

(C) understanding

(D) having understood

中譯

　　將近 75%患有系統性紅斑性狼瘡的病人經歷神經精神病症狀。但目前為止，有關紅斑性狼瘡對腦部產生影響時是怎樣一種機制，我們的理解仍很模糊。在找到真正的治療方式之前還有很長的一段路要走。

考題最前端

　　我們通常說我們對某項議題的了解非常有限，換成英文就是 What we understand about the issue is quite limited.也可以簡化一點，用動名詞來表示，Our understanding of the issue is quite limited.

　　如 果 熟 悉 這 類 句 型 的 變 換，那 麼 這 一 題 就 很 簡 單，是 our understanding of the mechanism。類 似 的 變 化 有，If you know something, you have knowledge of it.像是 knowledge of science 和 knowledge of music。

答案：(C)

動詞單複數動名詞當主詞

單 元概述

　　動名詞當主詞一定加單數動詞嗎？是否一定如此？

　　動名詞當主詞通常後面加單數動詞，如 Eating less is good for health.但如果有兩個動名詞作為主詞，後面就要用複數動詞，如 Reading and writing are both necessary for a student to develop his language skills. 然而，如果兩個動名詞主詞表達的是同一個概念，就要接單數動詞，如 Eating less and exercising more is good for health。

21-1 文法修行 Let's Go

Q21 請問你都怎麼理解動名詞主詞與動詞的一致性？有什麼更快的學習方式嗎？

「HOW」

■ 動名詞主詞與動詞的一致性基本上何一般主詞與動詞的一致性相同，如果 A 主詞和 B 主詞是不同的概念，兩個加起來就是複數的東西，所以自然後面接複數動詞。如果兩個主詞表達同一個概念，那就應視為單一的整體，後面要接單數動詞。例如，All work and no play makes Jack a dull boy.如何來看是否為同一概念？all work 表示一直在工作，就等於沒有任何娛樂 no play。

「Extra Bonus」

■ 另一常見的例子是 bread and butter （麵包塗奶油）

· Bread and butter is delicious. V.S. Bread and butter have become more expensive. （麵包和奶油）

「HOW」

■ 美國歌手雷斯科‧佛雷茲（Rascal Flatts）在〈最傷人的是〉（What Hurts The Most）這首歌中唱到：What hurts the most/Was being so close/And having so much to say/And watching you walk away/And never knowing/ What could have been（最傷人的是/離這麼近/有這麼多話要說/卻看著妳離開/永遠不知道/原來會怎樣）

■ 這裡用到好幾個作為主詞補語的動詞，有 being, having, watching, knowing，動名詞作為主詞，通常最多只多兩個，也就是 A+B，可是動詞名作為主詞補語，卻似乎不受限，這首歌就出現 A+B+C+D，似乎可以一直加下去。

「Extra Bonus」

■ 歌曲裡還有一句：And not seeing that loving you/Is what I was trying to do。這裡的 seeing 和 loving 都是動名詞，前者是主詞補語，後者是主詞。

Part
I
基礎實力養成篇

Part
II
進階文法修練篇

「HOW」

■ 動名詞作主詞可以讓主子變得比較有力，且顯得專業。例如，當我們說線上學習很方便時，通常會以 Online study is very convenient. 來表達，殊不知用動名詞來表達更為有力，即 Studying online is very convenient.一些比較複雜的句子也可以用動名詞來加以簡化，例如，If you swim in the winter, you can improve your immune system.可以改為 Swimming in the winter can improve your immune system.

■ 有時候可以和不定詞相互替換，但不見得每一個例子都能如此，例如，It is easier to learn a foreign language at a young age.和 Learning a foreign language at a young age is easier.基本上意思差不多。

「Extra Bonus」

■ 動名詞與不定詞之間的互換很有趣，最好學會。

- Learning a foreign language is hard. /It is hard to learn a foreign language./To learn a foreign language is hard.

21-2 考試一點靈

法加油站

- 動名詞也可以當形容詞，此時動詞的單複數要看動名詞所修飾的名詞。
  - Cooking lessons are fun. V.S. Cooking is fun.

- 判斷動名詞是否在形容後面的名詞，試問一下自己該名詞能否作為動詞的受詞，如果不行，那麼動名詞就是形容詞，真正的主詞是該名詞。如果行，動名詞才是真正的主詞，
  - Reading novels is interesting. （novels 是 read 的受詞）。

- 碰上複合動詞，要在第二字的後面加上 ing，例如，ice-skating, baby-sitting, mass-producing。
  - Roller-skating is exciting.

戰句

❶ If you want to slow aging, you might need to eat less. Researchers in the U.S. say eating less can slow the aging process of cells in the body. However, this-----is applicable only to laboratory mice for the moment. Researchers have yet to understand the mechanisms

underlying the aging process of human cells.

(A) found

(B) find

(C) finding

(D) has found

中譯

　　如果你想要延緩老化，可能要吃少一點。美國的研究人員説吃少一點可以延緩身體細胞的老化過程。然而，這個發現目前只適用於實驗室老鼠。研究人員仍有待了解人類細胞老化的背後機制。

考題最前端

　　動名詞作為主詞其實很好辨別，this 後面顯然是要接名詞，而動名詞 finding 是唯一符合條件的選項。這裡的 finding 相當於 discovery，是一種學術上的發現。this finding 也可以説成 their finding，也就是研究人員的發現。aging 也是動名詞，這裡做為動詞 slow 的受詞，後面 aging process 中的 aging 則是在形容 process，表示老化的過程。答案是 C。

答案：(C)

■ 當主詞由兩個意思緊密結合在一起的動名詞組成時，後面應該接單數動詞，但也有例外。

　・Running fast enough and keeping a steady pace is necessary to win the race./Running fast enough and keeping a steady pace are both necessary to win the race. （兩個句子都對，第二個句子因為主詞補語部位多加了一個 both，強調兩者，所以要用複數動詞）

■ 如果改成不定詞，那就一定要用單數動詞。

　・It is necessary to run fast enough and keep a steady pace to win the race.

■ 片語動詞也可能以動名詞型態作為主詞，後面只有單數動詞這一可能性，因為片語動詞的動名詞不可能成為形容詞。

　・Running after cars is dangerous.

實 戰句

❷ **People tend to believe that others will be influenced by their point of view over time, according to a series of new studies. The-----show that this "belief in a favorable future" exists in various contexts and cultures, helping understand some of the causes of the pervasive political and social polarization today.**

(A) discovery

(B) finding

(C) findings

(D) find

中譯

　　人們傾向於相信其他人終究會受到他們觀點的影響，這是根據一系列新研究。這些新發現顯示，這種「對有利未來的相信」存在於各種不同的環境和文化中，有助於了解現在政治及社會兩極化現象普遍存在的原因。

考題最前端

　　動名詞也可以有複數，一種發現是 finding，一種以上發現就是 findings。由於前一個句子已經用 a series of new studies 來表明有一系列的研究，它們有一共同的發現，但這一共同的發現是由個別不同的研究導出，所以可以用複數的形式來表示。但不是所有的動名詞都可以用複數形式，應該說類似的例子不算多，大部分還是以單數形式出現。finding 之所以能有複數，主要還是因為它已經被列為一種名詞。

答案：(C)

Part 2
進階文法修練篇

IBT 總分	90-105	105-120
學習規劃	分數段位於 90-105 左右的考生，除了掌握文法考點外，要多加強更進階的同義轉換跟答題技巧、熟悉 TPO 的出題方式。	分數段位於 105-120 左右的考生，除了掌握各文法考點，在聽說讀寫上都要具備相對地同義轉換能力，才能應對不同類型的聽力跟閱讀測驗。
延伸學習	**L** 訓練自己跟讀能力讓自己更專注在聽力訊息上。	**L** 多練習並充分掌握各類型的進階同義轉換。
	S 多開頭說並跟高分考生一起練習，或將口說答案請外籍老師修改，修正自己表達上的錯誤。	**S** 少使用教科書句子，並掌握道地口語詞彙，讓表達更貼近實際溝通。
	R 掌握進階篇的文法考點並應用於實戰句和 TPO 中。	**R** 除了掌握文法考點，仍需增加自己對各主題的閱讀量。
	W 注意語句連貫跟承轉詞的使用，讓文章更具邏輯性呈現。	**W** 學習各句式的表達，用豐富化句式表達論點。

不定詞和動名詞的區分

單 元概述

何謂不定詞？和動名詞有何差別？

不定詞、動名詞、分詞都是從動詞變來，最大的特色是不定詞前面一定要有 to，然後後面接原形動詞。不定詞和動名詞一樣保有部分的動詞特性，但可以當成名詞、形容詞、副詞使用，形成所謂的名詞片語、形容詞片語、副詞片語。不定詞作為名詞使用時，有時可以和動名詞相互替換，上一個單元已略作介紹。

22-1 文法修行 Let's Go

Q22 請問你怎麼理解不定詞和動名詞？有什麼更快的方式嗎？

「HOW」

■ 不定詞和動名詞一樣可以作為句子的主詞、動詞的受詞、及介系詞的受詞。大家經常看到一種不定詞，可是不見得都知道那是不定詞。

■ 例如，He likes to write. 這裡的 to write 就是不定詞，作為 like 的受詞，而 like 這個動詞後面也可以接動名詞，He likes writing.的意義和 He likes to write. 基本上一樣。不定詞 to write 和動名詞 writing 都是 like 的受詞。這樣一解釋，有沒有恍然大悟的感覺。

「**Extra Bonus**」

■ 有些動詞後面可以接動名詞，也可以接不定詞，像是 like，但有些動詞後面只能接不定詞，像是 agree, consent, decide, promise 等。

・He promised to help us.

「HOW」

■ 美國搖滾樂團魔力紅（Maroon 5）在這首〈投幣電話〉（Payphone）中唱到: I know it's hard to remember/The people we used to be/It's even harder to picture/That you're not here next to me
（我知道記得很難/我們以前的樣子/更難的是想像/妳不在這裡我的身邊）

■ It's even harder to picture that you're not here next to me.裡的 to picture 就是不定詞，是真正的主詞，前面的 it 是虛主詞。這種句型很常見，第一句 I know it's hard to remember 中的 to remember 也是不定詞，是 know 後面名詞子句的真主詞，it 則為虛主詞。

「Extra Bonus」

■ 這首歌一開頭的 I'm at a payphone trying to call home. 就用到不定詞 to call，作為動詞 try 的受詞。

「HOW」

■ 不定詞雖然有時可以和動名詞互換，但意思還是有差異。例如，It is difficult being a single parent.和 It is difficult to be a single parent. 在文法上都對，但前者用分詞表示實際的狀況，也就是當個單親家長很困難，而第二個句子是想像當個單親家長很困難。

■ 一些常用的諺語也用不定詞來表示假想的狀況，例如，To err is human, to forgive divine. 換成白話就是 If you err, you are human; if you forgive, you are divine.這些諺語都是用不定詞來表示，而不是動名詞。

「Extra Bonus」

■ 根據以上的原則，就比較好判斷不定詞和動名詞之間的微妙差別。

· Reading books is her hobby. 是正確的說法，不能說成 To read books is her hobby.

22-2 考試一點靈

文 法加油站

■ 不定詞比動名詞更具有動詞的效果，尤其是兩者前後出現在同一個句子時。

・I need to earn a better living.

■ 有些動詞後面雖然可以接不定詞也可以接動名詞，意義上雖然相同，但不定詞比較強調特殊的情況，動名詞則泛指一般狀況。

・I like to drink coffee in the morning. V.S. I like drinking coffee, but I also sometimes drink tea.

■ 同樣的規則可以套用到 prefer 這個常用的動詞上。

・When someone offers you a ride, you might choose to say, "I prefer to walk." V.S. I prefer walking.（指你平常都比較喜歡走路）

實 **戰句**

❶ Modern science allows researchers to---and move around the four biological compounds that make up DNA. Each polynucleotide chain in DNA is comparable to a necklace strung four types of beads, which are the four compounds known by the letters A, C, G and T.

(A) cutting

(B) cut

(C) have cut

(D) be cut

中譯

　　現代科學讓研究人員得以切割並移動組成 DNA 的四種生物化合物。DNA 裡的每個多核苷酸鍊可以比喻為一個由四種珠子串起的項鍊，這些珠子就是以 A、C、G、T 字母為代號的四個化合物。

考題最前端

　　有些動詞後面一定要接不定詞，allow 是其中之一，由於是及物動詞，必須先接受詞再接不定詞，形成 allow someone to do something 這個句型。Modern science allows researchers to cut and move around…. 這個句子剛好運用到 allow+受詞+不定詞句型，類似的還有 want+受詞+不定詞及 ask+受詞+不定詞。這些句型只能用不定詞，不能用動名詞。

答案：(B)

■ 就連 start 這個動詞也在接不定詞和動名詞時蘊藏著不同的意思。

· I started to speak, but she interrupted me on purpose. V.S. A small child usually starts speaking at the age of one.

■ 不定詞通常表示主動，而動名詞則表示被動。

· I need to clean my room. V.S. My room needs cleaning./My room needs to be cleaned.

■ 在某些動詞後面，不定詞表示未來的動作，動名詞則表示過去的動作。

· Remember to lock the door. V.S. I remember locking the door.

實 戰句

❷ "You can choose your friends, but you can't choose your family." It comes from U.S. writer Harper Lee's book "To---a Mockingbird." As an old saying goes, "Blood is thicker than water." In other words, family members will always be by your side while other people with no blood connection may not.

(A) killing

(B) killed

(C) have killed

(D) kill

中譯

　　「你能選擇你的朋友，卻不能選擇你的家人。」這句話來自美國作家 Harper Lee 的《梅岡城故事》一書。俗語說得好:「血濃於水」。換句話說，家人總會在你身邊，而其他沒有血緣的人可能不會。

考題最前端

　　之前討論過不定詞有假設的意味，而動名詞則是實際發生。當一部小說以 To Kill a Mockingbird 為名時，它的意義就不同於 Killing a Mockingbird，後者是告訴一個實際的經驗，而前者則是探討一個可能的狀況，mockingbird 在小說中代表人的純真，這種純真的逐漸喪失就是小說所要探討的主題，所以要用不定詞來指出可能發生的狀況。

答案：(D)

使役動詞後的動詞時態

　　何謂使役動詞？後面一定加原形動詞嗎？

　　使役動詞就是一種引發另一個行為的動詞，意思是叫某人、使某人或讓某人做一件事，常見的這類動詞有 *make, have, let, get, help*，它們大部分都是後面接受詞再接原形動詞（受詞為動詞意義上的主詞）或是接受詞再接過去分詞（受詞為接受動作的對象）。*get* 是唯一的例外，其受詞後面接的不是原形動詞，而是不定詞。

23-1 文法修行 Let's Go

Q23 請問你都怎麼記憶使役動詞的用法？有什麼更快的學習方式嗎？

「HOW」

■ 使役動詞的數目不多，應該很好記，但比較麻煩的是其中幾個也可以作為一般動詞用，所以有時會被搞錯。make, have, get 這三個動詞除了當使役動詞外，還可以作為一般動詞。

■ 例如，The teacher made his students read out the text. 這裡的 made 是使役動詞。Mr. Smith made a small toy for his son. 此時 made 就是一般動詞，意思是製作。使役動詞後面大多接原形動詞，但 get 除外。例如，Get someone to fix the door. 不能説 Get someone fix the door. 作為一般動詞時，get 就是得到或抓到的意思。

「Extra Bonus」

■ get 作為使役動詞時有説服的意思。

- I got him to stay for the night.（如果用 made him stay 就有比較強烈的意味）。

193

■ 電影《冰雪奇緣》（Frozen）中由艾迪娜·孟佐（Idina Menzel）所唱的主題曲〈隨它去吧〉（Let It Go）有這樣的歌詞：Let it go/Let it go/Can't hold it back anymore/Let it go/Let it go/Turn away and slam the door （隨它去吧隨它去吧/隨它去吧/再也擋不住了/隨它去吧/轉身關上門）

■ 我們可以看到 Let it go.這個短句被反覆地唱著，字面上看有點單調乏味，但搭配歌曲卻是好聽得很。這裡的 let 就是使役動詞。披頭四樂團（Beatles）也有一首類似的歌曲，英文叫做 Let It Be，和 Let It Go.有類似的意思，但不完全一樣。

「**Extra Bonus**」

■ Let it be.和 Let it go.基本上意思差不多，但前者比較強調 Leave the situation as it is.也是維持原樣，後者強調忘了，別再擔心了。

「HOW」

■ 使役動詞中，let 經常被用來形成祈使句，算是一種常見的句型。例如，Let us pray. 非正式用法可以寫成 Let's pray. 否定句的形式是 Do not let us forget to thank those who help us. 這是第一人稱複數的祈使句。

■ 第一人稱單數的祈使句常見的例子有 Let me think.和 Let me see.祈使句除了表達命令外，還提出建議。第三人稱祈使句比較具有命令性質，例如，Let the game begin.或 Let there be no doubt in your mind about my decision.

「Extra Bonus」

■ Let it go. 是隨它去的意思，注意有一看起來很像的慣用語 let go，是放手、鬆開的意思。

　・Hold the rope, and don't let go.

23-2 考試一點靈

文 法加油站

■ 使役動詞後面除了接原形動詞外，也可以接過去分詞（表示被動）或現在分詞（強調正在經歷的動作）。

・The man tried to make himself understood.

■ 後面用現在分詞就不是使役動詞原本所具有的使和讓的意思，而是陳述一種正在發生的現象。

・It is nice to have so many people playing in the park.

■ 電影裡常聽到有人說，"Am I making myself understood?"這句話通常是師長或長官在訓誡時用的，不要在日常生活中任意使用，這樣會使人反感。

・Have I made myself clear? 意思和 Am I making myself understood? 差不多。

實 戰句

❶ **Employees at a U.S. company volunteer to have chips----
-in their hands. Those who have these chips in their
hands can do many things just by waving their hands. It
is a new convenience unseen before.**

(A) implant

(B) implanting

(C) having implanted

(D) implanted

中譯

　　美國一家公司的職員自願在手裡植入晶片，手裡植入這些晶片的人只要揮揮手就能做許多事情，那是一種以前沒見過的新型便利。

考題最前端

　　這裡考的是 have something done 的句型，正常來說過去分詞後面比較少接詞語，這裡多加了 in your hands 這個介系詞片語，其功能是用來修飾 implanted。Implant 是植入某個東西，但植入到哪個部位呢？要用 in your hands 來表達部位。你也可以說，They have somebody implant chips in their hands. 這是主動形式，但比較累贅，不如被動式來得簡潔有力。答案是 D。

答案：(D)

文 ▶ 法加油站

■ have something done 和 get something done 是一種常用句型，但兩者在意義上不盡相同，也不能完全能相互替換。

· I had my hair cut. /I got my hair cut. /I had a haircut. /I got a haircut.

■ 若是表達請別人幫忙做某事或完成某事，have something done 等同於 get something done。如 I had my hair cut. /I got my hair cut.所示 I had my washing machine fixed. /I got my washing machine fixed. （通常是指找別人來修，如果是自己修，説 I fixed my washing machine.就好了）

■ 使役動詞 make 也有被動式，但後面要接不定詞。

· She was made to work on Sunday. /Her boss made her work on Sunday.

實 戰句

❷ **Recent studies found that doing meditation exercises can reduce stress in people suffering from anxiety and make them more-----. The studies also showed that meditation can make a person become more able to deal with stress.**

(A) produce

(B) productive

(C) produced

(D) production

中譯

　　最近的研究發現，冥想運動能減少患有焦慮症的人的壓力，讓他們更有生產力。這些研究也顯示，冥想能讓人變得更有能力處理壓力。

考題最前端

　　make 後面除了接原形動詞和過去分詞外，還可以接形容詞。這裡就是 make them more productive, 如果說成 make them become more productive，可能更好了解一點，但現在的英文講求簡潔，能省就省，所以 make+object+形容詞的句型越來越常見。後面句子裡的 make a person become more able to 則是標準的傳統用法，就是接原形動詞，再接形容詞補語。答案是 B。

答案：(B)

了解授與動詞

單 元概述

何謂授與動詞？怎樣區分直接和間接？

授與動詞是一種需要兩個受詞的動詞，一個受詞為直接受詞（*direct object*，簡稱 *DO*），另一個受詞為間接受詞（*indirect object*，簡稱 *IO*）。英文五大句型中的 S+V+O+O，就是授與動詞的基本句型。第一個 O 是 *IO*，通常指人，第二個 O 則是 *DO*，通常指物。這類動詞常見的有 *give, buy, tell*。

24-1 文法修行 Let's Go

Q24 請問你都怎麼記憶授與動詞？有什麼更快的學習方式嗎？

「HOW」

■ 授與動詞的最大特色是有兩個受詞，另一讓人感到困惑的地方是，只要把 DO 擺在前面，IO 擺在後面，就要加介系詞，有的是 for，有的是 to。什麼時候用 for，什麼時候用 to，要看前面的授與動詞而定。

■ 以 give 為例，就要用 to。例如，I gave her a book.（IO 在 DO 之前），若 DO 在 IO 之前，則要寫成 I gave a book to her. 再舉個例子，buy 後面就要接 for，而不是 to。I bought her a book. /I bought a book for her. 不同的授與動詞連接不同的介系詞。

「Extra Bonus」

■ 不少人會把 IO 和 DO 搞混，以為人才是直接受詞，物則為間接受詞，其實正好相反，因為買的或給的是物品，人只是接受者，只能當間接受詞。

201

「HOW」

■ 英國老牌搖滾樂團特拉格斯（The Troggs）有一首歌就叫做〈把它給我〉（Give It To Me），裡面唱到：Give it to me/Give it to me/All your love/All your love/Give it to me.（把它給我/把它給我/妳所有的愛/妳所有的愛/把它給我）

■ 歌詞很簡單，不斷重複 Give it to me.和 All your love，所以我們知道 it 指的是妳所有的愛，Give all your love to me.或 Give me all your love.也是同樣的意思，但不能說成 Give me it. 因為 it 是代名詞，只能擺在前面，後面接介系詞 to。

「Extra Bonus」

■ 有些慣用語看起來有點像是授與動詞句型，事實上不是，光看字面意思會鬧笑話。

・Give me a hand.不是給我一隻手，而是幫個忙。

「HOW」

■ 授與動詞的關鍵還是要搞清楚 IO 和 DO，為什麼人是間接受詞，而不是直接受詞。首先，直接受詞是文法上一定要存在的，而間接受詞卻不一定，例如，I bought a book.這樣就是一個完整的句子，卻不能說 I bought him.這樣會讓人以為你在從事人口販賣，是不對的說法。

■ 接下來有人會問，Why did you buy a book?如果是要送人，就要加上間接受詞，表示接受禮物的對象，此時就說，I bought a book for my friend Jack. 或 I bought my friend Jack a book.

「Extra Bonus」

■ 上一單元談到使役動詞，其中包括 make，它也可以作為授與動詞。

・My mother made a new shirt for me. /My other made me a new shirt.

24-2 考試一點靈

文 法加油站

- 顧名思義，授與動詞包括給予贈送之類動詞。比較常見的是 give 和 buy，比較沒那麼常見的有 hand, lend, offer, sell, send, teach, tell, write, cook, save, find, get, make, pick 等。有的後面接 to，有的接 for。

  · He handed me a glass of water./He handed a glass of water to me.

- 借東西也是一種授與行為，雖然不見得一定成功。

  · Could you lend me some money?

- 寫信、告訴、或寫東西都有一個對象，形成一種類似授與的互動。

  · She wrote me a letter. /She wrote a letter to me.

實 戰句

❶ **Recent studies found that men tend to give more tips----restaurant waiters than women. It was also found that people's political affiliation also affects their generosity with tips. Of course, people who earn more give bigger tips than those who earn less.**

(A) for

(B) to

(C) toward

(D) at

中譯

　　最近的研究發現，男人比女人更易於給更多的小費給餐廳侍者。同時發現的還有，政治傾向也影響到人們給小費的慷慨程度。當然，賺得比較多的人給的小費會比賺得比較少的人來得多。

考題最前端

　　給小費 give tips 是一種給予的行為，要接不定詞 to，不可能是 for，因為 for 帶有服務的意味。第一個句子的主詞是 recent studies，動詞 found，後面接 that 所引導的名詞子句，名詞子句中主詞是 men，動詞 tend，to give 是作為動詞受詞的不定詞，而 more tips 則是 give 的受詞。

答案：(B)

文 ▶ 法加油站

■ 授與動詞後面接介系詞 for 的通常有替人服務的味道，像是 cook, find, get, make。

- She cooked them a good dinner./She cooked a good dinner for them.

■ 授與動詞後面接介系詞 to 的，比較有提供某種物品或服務的意味。

- He offered me a job./He offered a job to me.

■ 如果還是怕弄錯介系詞，寫作文時盡量用不需要介系詞的 IO 在前句型，但還是要搞懂，因為選擇題會考。

- She gave me a present. 總是比 She gave a present to me. 來得簡單好記。

實 戰句

❷ Researchers say people treated for colon cancer can greatly reduce their death risk by following healthier lifestyles, such as eating more fruits and vegetables and taking exercise on a regular basis. It is a finding that----- much encouragement to colon cancer patients.

(A) borrows

(B) sends

(C) gives

(D) has

中譯

　　研究人員表示，接受大腸癌治療的人能藉著比較健康的生活方式，像是吃更多的蔬果及定期運動，來大幅減少死亡的危險。那是一個給了大腸癌患者很大鼓勵的發現。

考題最前端

　　英文現在趨向簡潔，動詞後面引導名詞子句的連接詞 that 經常被省略，這裡也是一樣。Researchers say people….本來應該是 Researchers say that people….，現在這種 that 通常會被省略，初學者最好養成保有 that 的習慣，因為一開始就刪掉 that，很可能以後會忘了本來有 that 的存在。答案是 C。

答案：(C)

了解感官動詞

單 元概述

何謂感官動詞？後面加原形動詞、現在分詞、過去分詞的差異在哪？

感官動詞也稱知覺動詞，也就是感覺器官的動詞，主要包括 hear, feel, watch, see,

look at, listen to, observe, notice 等動詞，構成主詞+動詞+受詞+原形動詞或分詞

（現在分詞或過去分詞）句型。另一類感官動詞，如 look, taste, smell, feel, sound,

則屬於連綴動詞的一種，後面不接受詞，而是補語，詳見連綴動詞單元。

25-1 文法修行 Let's Go

Q25 請問你都怎麼理解感官動詞？有什麼更快的學習方式嗎？

「HOW」

■ 感官動詞基本句型就是主詞+動詞+受詞+原形動詞或分詞（現在分詞或過去分詞）。比較麻煩的是什麼時候用原形動詞，什麼時候用分詞。舉例來說，I saw a man cross the street. 意思是我看到一個人穿越馬路。I saw a man crossing the street. 則表示我看到一個人正在穿越馬路。

■ 原形動詞代表完成的動作，現在分詞表示正在進行的動作。至於過去分詞，就是單純地表示被動的動作，例如，I heard my name called.換成白話，就是 Somebody called my name, and I heard it.

「Extra Bonus」

■ 如果表示連續的動作，那麼感官動詞後面就一定要用現在分詞。

・I saw her throwing stones at passer-by.（石頭是複數，要分次丟才能達到複數）

■ 美國歌手妮基‧布朗斯基（Nikki Blonsky）在〈我可以聽到鈴聲〉（I Can Hear The Bells）這首歌曲中唱到：Everybody says that a girl who looks like me can't /Win his love well just wait and see 'cause.../I can hear the bells/Just hear them chiming （每人都說我這樣一個女孩/不可能贏得他的愛，等著瞧，因為…/我可以聽到鈴聲/聽聽那悅耳的鈴聲）

■ 歌詞裡的 hear them chiming 表示正在聽到鈴聲，所以用現在分詞。這些鈴聲其實都是一個女孩幻想出來。

「**Extra Bonus**」

■ 宗教歌曲中常出現 hear the bells ringing 之類的歌詞，都是在表達一種喜悅的心態。也很常見到 see the angels coming。這些感官動詞後面都是加現在分詞。

「**HOW**」

■ 感官動詞也有被動式，從主動式改成被動式就要用到不定詞。例如，We never heard him say "thank you."被動式為 He was never heard to say "thank you." 此時就要以 heard 的受詞為主詞，原來的受格代名詞就要改為主格代名詞 he，原來的主詞 we 可以不用說，因為泛指一般人，而非特定的對象，這是被動式的特點。

■ 再舉一個例子，We saw him come. 的被動式是 He was seen to come. 這種形式和使役動詞的被動式差不多，複習一下，We made him do the job.改成被動式就是 He was made to do job by us.

「**Extra Bonus**」

■ 感官動詞主動式後面如果接的是現在分詞，改成被動式也還是要用現在分詞，而不是不定詞。
  ・Someone heard him crying./He was heard crying.

25-2 考試一點靈

文 法加油站

■ 基本上，感官動詞後面還是以加原形動詞為主，除非特別強調正在進行的動作，否則沒必要用現在分詞。

- I never saw him work. 這個 saw 後面不可能用現在分詞 working，因為前面用 never 表示了從來沒有。可是 I saw him work. 就可以說成 I saw him working.

■ 所以在使用感官動詞時，也要注意 never 之類頻率副詞也會限定感官動詞的用法。

- 某甲說，I never heard him talk in English. 某乙則反駁說，I heard him talking in English.

■ 不是所有的感官動詞都可以改成被動式，主要是指 see, hear, observe 這三個動詞，其他的則不適用，包括 feel, notice, watch, listen to, look at 等。

- He was observed to follow a lady closely. 這樣的句子比較難用主動式來表達，因為就是有人發現到他在跟蹤某位女士，不用特別指出是誰發現。

實 戰句

❶ Private drones-----flying near military bases could be at risk of capture or destruction. The U.S. military recently announced new guidelines about how to deal with civilian drones approaching military facilities.

(A) seen

(B) saw

(C) see

(D) having seen

中譯

　　被發現接近軍事基地的私有無人飛行器有遭到捕獲或摧毀的危險。美國軍方最近宣布新的指導方針來處理接近軍事設施的民用無人飛行器。

考題最前端

　　儘管熟悉感官動詞被動式的形式，但一碰到比較複雜的考題還是會慌到忘了。分析一下句型，第一個句子的主詞是 private drones，seen flying 是分詞片語，修飾主詞之用，原來是一個形容詞子句 that are seen flying，之前我們練習過形容詞子句改成分詞片語的方式，也就是去掉主格關係代名詞，再把一般動詞改成分詞，被動式則去掉 be 動詞保留過去分詞。答案是 A。

答案：(A)

文 法加油站

■ 當 see, hear, observe 這類感官動詞從主動式改為被動式時，後面可以接不定詞或現在分詞，不定詞暗示動作已經完成，現在分詞則表示動作持續一段時間。

- They saw a small child playing the middle of the road. /A small child was seen playing in the middle of the road. /A small child was seen to play in the middle of the road.

■ 感官動詞有些比較少人知道，像是 look at，它也是可以在後面接原形動詞或分詞。

- Look at him eating! /Look at him eat.

■ 感官動詞後面也可以被動語態的進行式，但很少見。

- I watched the tree being cut down. 一般來說 I watched the tree cut down. 就可以。

實 戰句

❷ **When a potential typhoon is seen-----be approaching Taiwan, local researchers will get themselves ready to get on a plane to fly into the typhoon to collect weather data. They are so-called typhoon hunters.**

(A) toward

(B) too

(C) to

(D) for

中譯

　　當一個可能成形的颱風被發現接近台灣時，當地研究人員就準備好搭上飛機飛入颱風收集氣候數據。他們是所謂的颱風獵人。

考題最前端

　　感官動詞的被動式除了接分詞外，也可以接不定詞。這題的不定詞還接上進行式，表示即將來臨的意味。potential 是潛在的、可能的意思，a potential typhoon 表示可能形成的颱風。台灣這個地區稱為 typhoon 的暴風，美國則稱為 hurricane，我們的 typhoon hunter 是取自美國的 hurricane hunter。

答案：(C)

了解助動詞

單 元概述

何謂助動詞？是在幫助動詞嗎？

助動詞本身沒有意義，主要功能是幫助動詞形成各種時態、語氣、疑問句、或否定句，常見的有 be, have, do，它們比較容易讓人搞不清楚的地方是也可以作為一般動詞用。除了這幾個助動詞外，還有情態助動詞，包括 will, would, shall, should, can, could, may, might, must, ought to，被用來表示：可能性、必要、許可、意圖、或能力。

26-1 文法修行 Let's Go

Q26 請問你都怎麼記憶助動詞？有什麼更快的學習方式嗎？

「HOW」

■ 助動詞的數目實在不少，想在一時之間完全搞懂實在不容易。情態助動詞和一般助動詞都不能獨立存在，必須與其他動詞再一起才能發揮作用。例如，I sing. 表示唱歌的動作。I can sing. 表示有歌唱的能力。I am singing. 這裡的 be 動詞是助動詞，和後面的現在分詞 singing 形成現在進行式。

■ 只有情態助動詞 can 表示能力，be 助動詞只是形成一個正在進行的動作，沒有能不能或好不好的問題。

「Extra Bonus」

■ 情態助動詞沒有人稱變化，不管主詞是第幾人稱，形式都一樣。

· He can sing. 不能寫成 He cans sing.

「HOW」

■ 披頭四樂團（Beatles）在〈我願意〉（I Will）這首歌中唱到：And when at last I find you/Your song will fill the air/Sing it loud so I can hear you/Make it easy to be near you （所以最後當我找到妳/妳的歌聲將充滿整個空氣/大聲唱出我才能聽到妳/讓我容易接近妳）

■ 除了歌名有助動詞外，歌詞裡的 Your song will fill the air. 也有 will。這兩個 will 的意思不完全一樣，第一個表示意願，第二個表示未來。一個是我願意，另一個是妳的歌聲將充滿整個空氣。

「Extra Bonus」

■ 除了 will 外，shall 也可以表示未來。通常第一人稱 I/we 要用 shall 來表示未來，但現代美語則用 will 來取代 shall。
  · I will be home soon./I shall be home soon.

「HOW」

■ 剛學英文時，我們搞不懂 can 和 may 之間的差別，每次問老師，Can I go to the bathroom? 老師總會糾正說，May I go to the bathroom? 才對。學了一陣子後才知道 can 是表示能力，上廁所不是能力問題，得到老師的許可就要用 may。助動詞用錯也會要人命，

■ 一個老中跌入水塘中，不斷地喊著，I will drown. Nobody shall save me. 可是老外聽了卻都不幫忙，因為他說的是我願意淹死，不要有人來救我。他應該這麼說才對： I shall drown. Nobody will save me. 我快要淹死了，可是卻沒有人願意救我。

「Extra Bonus」

■ 請求許可通常以 may 為主，但也有人用 can，但還是以 may 為主流。

・May I have your attention, please? 也有人說 Can I have your attention, please?

26-2 考試一點靈

文 法加油站

- 助動詞雖然有過去式，像是 may 的 might，can 的 could，will 的 would，但這些過去式有時不是表示時態，而是可能性、要求、或意願。

  - He may come tomorrow.和 He might come tomorrow. 都是表示推測，might 的可能性較低。

- 如果表示猜測，助動詞的肯定程度排名如下：must, will/would, should/ought to, can/could/may/might。must 的可能性最大，might 的可能性最小。絕不是則為 can't。

  - The man must be the one the police are looking for.語氣比 The man might be the one the police are looking for. 強多了。

- 表示對過去事實的假設時，可以用 might 和 could。

  - He was very careless when crossing the road. He might/could have been killed.

實 戰句

❶ **Patents enable products and services to be created that otherwise-----not be developed at all. But the question is that the grant of patent rights is too broad now. Pharmaceutical companies owning patents tend to make claims that are too far-reaching.**

(A) should

(B) would

(C) shall

(D) must

中譯

　　專利可以讓本來無法發展出來的產品和服務得以問世，但問題是專利的給予過於廣泛。擁有專利的製藥公司易於提出過於廣泛的要求。

考題最前端

　　would 可以構成假設語氣，與現在事實相反的用 would+原形動詞，與過去事實相反的則用 would+have+過去分詞。otherwise（否則，不然）的出現就是在引出一個假設的狀況（事實上並沒有發生）。因為有專利的給予，才讓一些產品和服務得以問世，不然的話，它們根本就發展出來。有了專利的保障，製藥公司才敢花大錢下去投資。答案是 B。

答案：(B)

文 法加油站

■ would 作為情態助動詞時不是 will 的過去式,而是表示意願、客氣的提議或請求,will 也有同樣的意思,但 would 的語氣比較和緩。

　・Would/Will you please wait for a moment?

■ would like to 是一種慣用語,意思是 want to 或 love to,一種客氣的說法。

　・I would like(I'd like)to have some tea.

■ 動詞 hope, expect, believe 表達可能實現的期待,後面的句子連帶要用 will 而不是 would,因為 would 代表可能性沒那麼高。

　・We hope that your dream will come true.如果用 would,當事人會很難過。

實戰句

❷ **The value of bitcoin, a virtual currency, has jumped to a record high in August 2017, reaching US$3,451.86 per coin. The market value of all bitcoins in the world----- now surpassed US$56 billion.**

(A) have

(B) had

(C) has

(D) does

中譯

　　虛擬貨幣比特幣的價值於 2017 年 8 月來到最高點，每枚比特幣可值 3451.86 美元。全世界比特幣的市值現在已經超過 560 億美元。

考題最前端

　　助動詞 have 可以和過去分詞構成完成式，如 has done, have done, had done。第一個句子 has jumped 已經給了一個提示，表示用到了現在完成式。第二個句子又是在講現在超過什麼，很明顯地要用現在現在完成式，主詞是 market value，助動詞要用第三人稱單數的 has。答案是 C。

答案：(C)

了解連綴動詞

何謂連綴動詞？和感官動詞的差別在哪呢？

連綴動詞不是一般動詞，功用不在表達動作，而是描述主詞的狀態，作為主詞和補語之間的連結。最常見的連綴動詞是 be 動詞，它本身無法表達動作，只是帶出後面的主詞補語（通常是形容詞和名詞）。有些感官動詞，如 taste, smell, look, sound, feel, 也屬於連綴動詞，它們和前面單元所介紹的 see, hear 之類感官動詞，see 這類動詞無法作為連綴動詞，只能接受詞再接原形動詞或分詞。

27-1 文法修行 Let's Go

Q27 請問你都怎麼記憶連綴動詞？有什麼更快的學習方式嗎？

「**HOW**」

■ 連綴動詞的句型很單純，就是後面接補語，而補語大多是形容詞或名詞，間或也有代名詞。be 動詞是最常見的連綴動詞，同學可能會感到疑惑，因為之前不是介紹 be 為助動詞嗎？怎麼現在又成了連綴動詞？

■ be 作為助動詞時，後面要接現在分詞或過去分詞形成進行式或被動式，真正的動詞是分詞，be 只是擔任協助的角色，所以才叫做助動詞。而作為連綴動詞，be 後面接的是補語，不是分詞形式的動詞，補語是補充說明的詞語，無法表達動作。

「**Extra Bonus**」

■ 簡單舉一個例子，I am a student. 這個句子裡 be 動詞是連綴動詞，而 I am studying.裡的 be 動詞則是助動詞，真正的動詞是 studying.

「HOW」

■ 加拿大殲滅者樂團（Annihilator）在〈在我聽起來很好〉（Sounds Good To Me）這首歌中唱到：Dream away don't wait for the night/ 'Cause any old time at all sounds good to me/ Dream away, everything's alright/I hope it sounds good to you, sounds good to me（進入夢鄉，不用等到晚上/因為任何老時光在我聽起來都很好/進入夢鄉，萬無問題/我希望在你聽起來很好，在我聽起來很好）

■ 歌詞裡的 sound 就是連綴動詞，後面接形容詞 good 作為補語。日常生活中常聽人說，It sounds good to me. 意思是在我聽起來很好或不錯，表示接受你的提議或意見。

「Extra Bonus」

■ 也有人說 It sounds good for me. 這是怎麼回事？不是應該用 to 嗎？其實用 for 也可以，只是意義不一樣，用 to 的意思是在我看來很好，用 for 是表示對我有好處。

「HOW」

■ 作為連綴動詞的感官動詞大多能在後面加一個介系詞 like，介系詞後面再接名詞作為比較之用。例如，He looked like the man we saw yesterday. 或 This song sounds like the song we heard before.也可以用 feel like, smell like, taste like 來表達類似的比較。

■ 現在口語化的說法會在 like 後面連一個句子，像是 It is so hot today. I feel like I am melting. 這樣的說法在前面的單元介紹過，由於正式的書寫文章尚未全面接納這種用法，因為 like 是介系詞，不是連接詞，無法帶出一個句子。同學們知道有這個口語上的用法就好。

「Extra Bonus」

■ 當我們說他看起來高興，英文是 He looks happy. 而不是 He looks like happy. 因為 like 是介系詞，後面不能直接接形容詞。He looks like a happy person.就沒錯了。

27-2 考試一點靈

文 法加油站

■ 連綴動詞還包括一些表示狀態或狀態變化的動詞，包括 seem, turn, go, grow, prove, get, appear, remain, become 等。

· He seems（to be）happy. /He appears（to be）happy.

■ 前述動詞有的雖然後面和連綴動詞一樣接形容詞，但它們通常省略了 to be，有人習慣保留 to be，有人習慣省略，兩者都對。seem 後面還可以接 as if 或 as though，引導出一個子句。這類動詞中會這樣用的，通常只有 seem 和 appear。

· The children seemed as if（as though）they were tired.

■ 這類動詞中另一常用的是 get，後面多半接形容詞，像是 get angry, get hungry, get tired, get better。如果後面要接一個名詞，就要用到不定詞（grow 也有類似的用法）。

· How did you get to be a street artist?

實 戰句

❶ **In many countries, especially those in Europe, there is no custom of napping. However, a Spanish company has opened the first public napping space in Madrid. The idea-----to work well with the culture of Spain, where people usually take a nap in the afternoon.**

(A) appear

(B) appeared

(C) appears

(D) appearing

中譯

　　在許多國家，特別是歐洲國家，並沒有午睡這個習慣。然而，一家西班牙公司在馬德里開了第一個公眾午睡空間，這個構想似乎符合西班牙的文化，那裡的人通常會睡午覺。

考題最前端

　　appear 和 seem 一樣可以在後面接 to be，但如果後面是形容詞，to be 通常會被省略掉，直接說 appear tired 或 seem tired 就可以。不過如果後面要連接另一個動詞，就一定要保留 to，像是考題中的 The idea appears to work well….，沒辦法說成 appears work 或 appears working，只有不定詞才是正確的用法。

答案：(C)

文 法加油站

■ become 也是很常見，後面可以接形容詞，也可以接名詞，接形容詞時等同於 turn，但 turn 後面通常不接名詞。

· It was becoming cold. /It was turning cold.

■ remain 這個動詞在用法上幾乎和 be 動詞一樣，後面可以接形容詞、名詞、介系詞片語，不定詞片語等，把它的位置用 be 填上，也都能通，但兩者的意思還是不一樣。

· The patient still remains in bed. 或 Many things remain to be done.

■ taste 和 smell 這兩個動詞後面還可以接 of，再接名詞，表達出類似 like 的意思。

· The tea tastes of mint.

實 戰句

❷ U.S. scientists have calculated the total amount of plastic items ever made on this planet. The number seems-----around 8 billion tons. The big issue is that these plastic items, usually used only for short periods before being discarded, have now become a major source of waste polluting the environment.

(A) to

(B) be

(C) been

(D) to be

中譯

　　美國科學家把這個星球製造出來的塑膠製品總量做了一個統計，數量似乎在 80 億公噸左右。現在一大議題是，這些通常只用很短一段時間就被丟棄的塑膠製品，現在已經成為汙染環境的一個主要廢棄物來源。

考題最前端

　　seem to be 比較常出現在正式或學術性文章，一般文章或日常對話只要用到 He seems happy. 這樣簡單的句型即可。這裡把 seem 換成 appear 也可以，因為兩者不但意思相近，連用法也相近。如果很確定數字，直接用 be 動詞就好，seem 和 appear 是用來表示大概的意思，所以後面數字前面才加了一個 around。答案是 D。

答案：(D)

熟悉量詞

單 元概述

　　何謂量詞？有何特色？

　　量詞就是表示數量的詞，是一種限定詞，所謂限定詞是放在名詞用來限定名詞的詞，有點像是形容詞，但也不盡然。限定詞包括冠詞（a, an, the）、量詞和代名形容詞。這個單元只討論量詞。針對可數名詞與不可數名詞，各有不同的量詞，many, few, a few 用在可數名詞，much, little, a little 則用在不可數名詞。some, any, enough, lots of 則可以同時用在可數與不可數名詞。

28-1 文法修行 Let's Go

Q28 請問你都怎麼記憶量詞？有什麼更快的學習方式嗎？

「HOW」

■ 量詞雖然很多，但最關鍵的還是要搞清楚後面的名詞是可數還是不可數，如果連可數不可數都不清楚，那就白搭了。

■ 用在不可數名詞的有 much, a little/little/very little, a bit（of）, a great deal of, a large amount of, a large quantity of。

■ 用在可數名詞的有 many, a few/few/very few, a number（of）, several, a large number of, a great number of, a majority of。

■ 兩者皆可用的有 all, enough, more/most, less/least, no/none, not any, some, any, a lot of, lots of, plenty of。從這些詞可看出，只要有 much 和 little，就是指不可數，只要有 many 和 few（不管是 a few 還是 very few），就是指可數。先記這些，因為它們出現的頻率最高。

「Extra Bonus」

■ 比較有趣的是，到了比較級和最高級，可數和不可數名詞都適用，它們包括 more/most、less/least。

· If we have more visitors, we can earn more money.

「HOW」

■ 英國老牌歌手菲爾‧柯林斯（Phil Collins）在 1980 年代推出一首膾炙人口的歌，叫做〈再一個夜晚〉（One More Night），其中唱到：One more night, one more night/I've been trying oh so long to let you know/Let you know how I feel/And if I stumble if I fall, just help me back/So I can make you see（再一個夜晚，再一個夜晚/我努力了很久，只想讓妳知道/讓妳知道我的感受/如果我摔倒跌倒，幫我一下就好/這樣我就能讓妳明白）

■ 再一個夜晚是 one more night，如果是再兩個夜晚呢？答案是 two more nights，其他依此類推。

「Extra Bonus」

■ 有人會問，可不可以說 one night more？其實是可以的，因為文法上無誤，但一般人比較常說 one more night 或 one more day。

「HOW」

■ 表示兩個人或事物的量詞有 both, either, neither，它們同時也可以作為代名詞，由它們的變化可以清楚看出量詞的用法。例如，The convenience store was closed./The convenience store wasn't open./I don't think the convenience store was open. 這三個句子都在指一間超商。改成兩間超商就變成，Both the convenience stores were closed./Neither of the convenience stores was open./I don't think either of the convenience stores was open.

■ 如果有兩間以上超商，就要說，All the convenience stores were closed./None of the convenience stores were open./I don't think any of the convenience stores were open. 從這些句型變化可以了解量詞與代名詞及動詞單複數之間的關係。

「Extra Bonus」

■ 用 every 和 each 也可以表示所有，但後面要接單數名詞。如果用 all，後面就要接複數名詞。

· Each shop was crowded with customers. /All the shops were crowded with customers.

28-2 考試一點靈

文 法加油站

- 對於不可數名詞，最常用到的量詞是 much, a little, little, a bit of, a lot of, lots of, some
  - When you earn much/a lot of/lots of money, you won't think it is enough.

- 最常用到可數名詞的量詞有 many, a few, few, several, some, a lot of, lots of
  - He has many books in his house, but he has read only a few of them.

- 同時適用可數和不可數名詞的量詞有 all, enough, more/most, less/none, some, any, a lot of, lots of, plenty of。
  - All of my friends complain about not having enough money because all their money is tied up in long-term investments.

實 戰句

❶ **Japanese carmaker Mazda has successfully developed a more efficient petrol engine, a compression ignition engine, as other competitors steer toward electric**

vehicles. It plans to sell cars with the new engine in two years. But it has-----plans to supply the new engine to other carmakers that might become its competitors.

(A) none

(B) no

(C) any

(D) little

中譯

　　日本車廠馬自達已經成功開發出一款更有效的汽油引擎，那是一種壓縮點火引擎，與此同時，其他競爭者正朝電動汽車的方向發展。馬自達計畫在兩年上市裝配該引擎的汽車，但沒有計畫提供新引擎給其他可能成為競爭對手的車廠。

考題最前端

　　量詞 no 和 none 後面可以接可數名詞，也可以接不可數名詞。這裡考的就是 no，no 後面接可數名詞時要用複數名詞，接不可數名詞時要用單數名詞。所以 no plans 才對。說成 I has no intention of selling cars....也行，此時 no 後面接的是抽象名詞，是不可數名詞，所以要用單數。

答案：(B)

文 法加油站

■ a 和 one 都可以用來指一個人或物，意思差不多，但前者強調一個，後者表示好幾個人或事物中的一個。

- A feature of the book is concision and precision. 和 One feature of the book is concision and precision. 的差別在於後者強調幾個特色中的一個，而前者只提那一個特色。

■ 還有表示「群」的量詞，像是 a group/crowd of people, a herd of cattle/elephants, a flock of sheep/birds/geese, a brood of chickens, a swarm of insects, a school of fish, a pack of dogs, a gang of bandits, a flight of stairs 等。

- A crowd of people was standing at the entrance to the museum./A crowd of people were standing at the entrance to the museum. 兩個句子都對，前者是把那群人視為一個整體，所以用單數動詞，後者把那群人視為一群個體，所以用複數動詞。

■ 可以把不可數名詞變成可數名詞，這樣就能搭配更多的量詞。例如，a cup of coffee, a glass of wine, a piece of advice, a loaf of bread, a slice of cheese, a strand of hair。

- Would you like some water?/Would you like a glass of water?兩種說法都行。

實 戰句

❷ Recent research done by Internet search giant Google found that cyber-thieves earned at least US$25 million from ransomware in the last two years. Google created-----of virtual ransomware victims to understand how cyber-thieves operated.

(A) hundred

(B) thousand

(C) thousands

(D) ten

中譯

　　網路搜尋引擎巨擘谷歌最近研究發現，網路小偷過去兩年經由勒索軟體賺了至少 2500 萬美元。谷歌製造出數千個虛擬勒索軟體受害者來了解網路小偷是如何運作。

考題最前端

　　量詞中另一種常見的是 hundreds of, thousands of, millions of, dozens of, scores of，後面理所當然要接可數名詞。有趣的是沒有 tens of 這個說法，數十個通常用 dozens of 來表示，不能說成 tens of，不過卻有 tens of thousands of，意思是數萬。為什麼不能用 tens of 來表示數十個？語言是約定俗成，目前的規定就是這樣。答案是 C。

答案：(C)

熟悉假設語氣

單 元概述

何謂假設語氣？是不是都要用到 if 條件句？

假設語氣是動詞形式的一種，用來表達與事實相反的願望、建議、命令、或狀況，通常和 if 條件句搭配使用，但也可以不用 if 條件句。像是常用 wish 來表達與事實相反的願望，此時就不用 if 條件句。as if 和 as though 也可以引導出假設語氣的副詞子句，但屬於比較誇飾的說法。

29-1 文法修行 Let's Go

Q29 請問你都怎麼記憶假設語氣？有什麼更快的學習方式嗎？

「HOW」

■ 假設語氣主要表達兩種狀況，一是與現在或未來事實相反的願望，另一是與過去事實相反的願望。第一種狀況用到 be 動詞時，不分人稱和單複數，都要用 were。

■ 而第二種狀況則是不分人稱和單複數，都要用過去完成式（had+過去分詞）。用 wish 來表達假設語氣基本上就是這兩種變化，如果搭配 if 條件句，就會比較複雜，但還是不出與現在或未來事實相反及與過去事實相反這兩種變化。

「**Extra Bonus**」

■ 以 wish 來表達假設語氣。

・ I wish I were rich.（I am not rich.）

・ I wish I had not made the mistake.（I made the mistake.）

「HOW」

■ 知名的美國樂團芝加哥（Chicago）有一首歌曲叫做〈如果妳現在離開我〉（If You Leave Me Now），歌詞中用到 if 條件句：If you leave me now, you'll take away the biggest part of me/Baby, please don't go.（如果妳現在離開我，你將帶走我最大的一部分/寶貝，請不要走）。

■ 這裡的 if 條件句用的都是簡單現在式，表達的不是與現在、未來、或過去事實相反的狀況，而是一種可能實現的假設。也就是說，如果女方真的離開，男方會遭受很大的打擊。

「Extra Bonus」

■ 從 if 條件句的動詞時態，可以看出假設狀況的可能性。
  - If I have enough money, I will buy the car.（有可能實現）
  - If I had enough money, I would buy the car.（不太可能實現）
  - If I had had enough money, I would have bought the car.（完全不可能實現）

「**HOW**」

■ 用 if 條件句來表達與現在或未來事實相反的假設時，if 子句用過去式（were/did），主要子句則用助動詞過去式（would, might, could, should），再接原形動詞。

■ 用 if 條件句來表達與過去事實相反的假設時，if 子句用過去完成式，主要子句則用助動詞過去式（would, might, could, should），再接 have+過去分詞。看起來要比 wish 句型複雜了許多，但謹記一個原則，與過去事實相反的假設，不管是 if 子句還是主要子句，都要用到完成式，其中一個是過去完成式，另一個則是助動詞所帶出的完成式。

「**Extra Bonus**」

■ 記住 if 子句和主要子句的時間點和時態要一致。
  ・If I had had enough money, I would buy the car. （這樣說是錯的，要 would have bought 才對）。

243

29-2 考試一點靈

文 法加油站

■ 只要用到 wish 動詞，後面的子句就要用到假設語氣。

 · I wish I knew her name.

■ wish 本身的時態並不影響到後面子句是要用過去式還是過去完成式。

■ I wish she had accepted my suggestion.和 I wished she accepted my suggestion.這兩句子都對，前一個句子的時間點是在現在，所表達是與當時的過去相反的事實，第二個句子的時間點在過去，所表達的是過去的那個當下相反的事實。

■ wish 子句也可以用 could 和 would 這兩個助動詞來表達願望。

 · I wish I could play tennis as well as you.

實 戰句

❶ A U.S. technology firm has developed a drone capable of aiming and firing at hostile targets while flying in mid-air. A drone is formally called an unmanned aerial vehicle (UAV). The Tikad drone, armed with a machine-gun and a grenade launcher, is expected to reduce

casualties in an armed conflict, but-----in the wrong hands, it would be used against innocent people as well.

(A) it

(B) if

(C) only

(D) though

中譯

　　一家美國科技公司開發出一種能在飛行途中對敵對目標進行瞄準和射擊的無人機。無人機的正式名稱為無人飛行器。這款 Tikad 無人機裝備了機關槍和榴彈發射器，預期能在武裝衝突中減少傷亡，但如果落入居心不良的人的手中，就會被用來對付無辜之人。

考題最前端

　　if 條件句可以簡化成片語形式，只要 if 子句和主要子句的主詞相同，就可以省略

　　if 子句的主詞和動詞（be 動詞去掉，一般動詞改成分詞）。這個句子本來是： If it were in the wrong hands, it would be used against innocent people as well.句子裡的 it 都是指無人機，所以可以省略 if 子句中的 it，使整個 if 子句成為片語。所以答案是 B。

答案：(B)

文 法加油站

■ as if 所開頭的子句，表達的是與事實相反的狀況，也是要用假設語氣。

- He talks as if he knew everything.

■ as though 的意思和 as if 一樣，可以彼此互換。

- She looks as though she had done something wrong.

■ 也可以用 if only 來表達假設語氣，if only 子句通常獨立存在。

- If only I had arrived earlier.

實 戰句

❷ **Scientists are very worried that the melting of the Greenland ice sheet could accelerate and raise sea levels more than expected. Scientists are very worried about climate change. If all the ice in Greenland melted, the global sea level-----rise by 7 meters.**

(A) will

(B) would

(C) shall

(D) is

中譯

　　科學家非常擔心格陵蘭冰層會加速融化，使海平面上升幅度超過預期。科學家非常擔心氣候變遷。如果格陵蘭的冰全都融化，全球的海平面將上升 7 公尺。

考題最前端

　　這題要考的就是與現在或未來事實相反的假設。雖然格陵蘭冰層融化是事實，但沒有到全部融化的地步，所以 if 子句設定的是與現在或未來事實相反的狀況，主要子句就要用助動詞的過去式，再接原形動詞。如果答案選項有 could，那麼 would 就不會是唯一的選擇，因為 could 表達一種可能性。

答案：(B)

熟悉被動語態

單 元概述

何謂被動語態？只要在 be 動詞後面加過去分詞嗎？

英文有主動語態和被動語態，主動語態就是主詞為動詞的執行者，被動語態是主詞為動詞的接受者。一般文章還是以主動語態為主，但在學習英文過程仍要學習被動語態，因為有時會用到。被動語態基本上就是 be 動詞加過去分詞，有時候 be 動詞可以用 get 代替。

30-1 文法修行 Let's Go

Q30 請問你都怎麼記憶被動語態？有什麼更快的學習方式嗎？

「HOW」

■ 主動語態是施行動作的人或物擺在句子的前面，被動語態是接收動作的人或物擺在句子的前面，施行動作者在句子後面，前面要加上介系詞 by。例如：He bought a book./A book was bought by him. 由於 by 是介系詞，後面要接受格代名詞 him，而不是主格的 he。這是被動式的基本形式，不過經常出現的狀況是施行動作者被省略，因為重點在接收動作的人或物，像是 it is said that 這個句型，重點在於傳說的內容，而不是誰說的。

「Extra Bonus」

■ 和 it is said that 類似的句型還有 it is believed/though/considered/supposed/rumored/expected/known/alleged that，這些句型很好用，也很常見，一定要熟悉才行。

249

「**HOW**」

■ 英國知名歌手愛黛兒（Adele）在〈像你的某個人〉（Someone Like You）這首歌中唱到: I heard that you're settled down/That you found a girl and you're married now （我聽説你已經安頓下來/你找了一個女孩且現在已經結婚了）

■ 歌詞中的 be settled down 其實用主動語態的 settle down 就可以，不過現在口語上不少人用 be settled down 來代替 settle down，意思都是安頓下來。後面的 be married 就是標準的被動式，也可以用 get married 來表示，帶兩者的意思不盡相同，前者表示一個狀態，後面表達一個過程和動作。

「**Extra Bonus**」

■ 同一首歌中還有段：I had hoped you'd see my face/And that you'd be reminded that for me （我曾經希望你會看到我的臉/那樣你就會被提醒到我）裡面的 be reminded 用得很漂亮。

「HOW」

■ 被動語態的基本形式是 be 動詞+過去分詞，但還有許多種變化，像是含助動詞的被動語態、進行式的被動語態、完成式的被動語態、否定句的被動語態、及疑問句的被動語態。聽起來有點複雜，但只要根據句型的要求來做相對應的變化即可。

■ 例如：The cake can be eaten./The cake is being eaten./The cake has been eaten./The cake has not been eaten./Has the cake been eaten? 這些被動式的變化都是隨著句型而定，所以不能單純地認為只有 be 動詞+過去分詞這個形式。

「Extra Bonus」

■ 疑問句的被動語態還包括使用疑問詞的問句。

· Who was this song written for?

30-2 考試一點靈

文 法加油站

■ 某些情況被動式是比較常用的形式，像是施行動作者不明時。

· The wall paintings were made in the Han Dynasty.

■ 或是施行動作者不那麼重要或相關時。

· The new measure will be launched on an experimental basis.

■ 或是表達一般性的真理時。

· Rules are made to be broken.

實 戰句

❶ **Former U.S. Vice President Al Gore, now a leading voice in the fight against climate change, has launched his latest eco-movie, An Inconvenient Sequel. He hopes that the film will persuade people that the climate can be-----if everybody tries hard enough.**

(A) saven

(B) save

(C) saved

(D) been saved

中譯

　　現已成為對抗氣候變遷領導人物之一的美國前副總統高爾，推出最新製作的環保電影《不願面對的真相 2》。他希望這部電影能說服大家，只要每人做足努力，還是可以拯救氣候。

考題最前端

　　這題不但考 if 條件句，也測驗被動式。He hopes 後面接一個 that 所引導的名詞子句，這個名詞子句中的主詞是 film，助動詞 will 是因為 hope 這個動詞後面的子句要用 will 來表達可以實現的願望，動詞 persuade 後面接一個 that 子句，這個子句中又有 if 條件句型，這個條件句是表達可以實現的願望，所以都用簡單現在式。save 的過去分詞是 saved，所以答案是 C。

答案：(C)

文 法加油站

■ 當接收動作者才是句子的重點時，被動式是比較好的表達方式。

· Green power that is produced by new power generation technologies will become the norm in the future.

■ 及物動詞才有被動語態，不及物動詞和連綴動詞沒有被動語態。

· She sings very well.（不能改成被動式，因為沒有受詞，也就是沒有接收動作者）

■ 有些句型慣用被動式，如之前提過的 it is said that。

· You are supposed to behave properly.

實 戰句

❷ **Scientists in Oregon successfully fixed a disease-carrying gene in human embryos. It was the first time this has been-----. The scientists used gene editing to correct a disease-causing mutation in human embryos.**

(A) do

(B) did

(C) doing

(D) done

中譯

　　奧瑞岡州的科學家成功地修復人類胚胎中一種帶病基因。這樣的成功嘗試是第一次。這些科學家用基因剪輯的方式修正人類胚胎中導致疾病的突變。

考題最前端

　　這裡考的是完成式的被動語態，It was the first time this has been done.中的 this 是指前面句子所提的事情，it is the first time that（that 可以省略）句型要在 that 所引導的子句中用現在完成式。問題是。這裡是 It was the first time 而不是 It is the first time，有人或許會問這樣後面還接現在完成式嗎？答案是肯定的，因為 it was the first time 是指當時那件事，而那件事持續到現在都是世界的第一次。所以答案是 D。

答案：(D)

熟悉疑問句

單 元概述

何謂疑問句?

顧名思義,疑問句表達一種疑問,可分為幾種類型:Yes/No 疑問句、疑問詞開頭的疑問句、選擇性疑問句、附加問句。第一和第三種類型通常用助動詞 do 起頭,第二類型則要用疑問代名詞(who, what, which)或疑問副(when/where/why/how)。第四類型是附加在直述句後面的問句,通常用 be 和 do 這兩種助動詞起頭。

31-1 文法修行 Let's Go

Q31 請問你都怎麼理解疑問句？有什麼更快的學習方式嗎？

「**HOW**」

■ 我們經常碰到疑問句，像是 Yes/No 疑問句: Do you like reading? 或 Is it raining? 疑問詞開頭的疑問句也很多，例如: Why did you do that? 選擇性疑問句出現的機率較小，例如：Do you want beef noodle or fried rice?

■ 至於附加問句，美國人比較少用，但英國人很常用，所以還是得熟悉一下，例如：You like it, don't you? 或 It is very cold today, isn't it?這些是我們常見的疑問句，不太難，也不是很複雜，但還是有很複雜的疑問句，不見得那麼好懂。

「**Extra Bonus**」

■ 補充說明，Yes/No 疑問句除了 be 和 do 這兩個助動詞外，也用到 have（構成完成式）和情態助動詞，像是 can。

・Have you finished your homework?

「HOW」

■ 2016 年獲得諾貝爾文學獎的美國民謠歌手巴布‧狄倫（Bob Dylan）在他這首著名的〈隨風而逝〉（Blowin' In The Wind）歌曲中唱到: How many roads must a man walk down/Before you call him a man?/How many seas must a white dove sail/Before she sleeps in the sand? （一個男人要走多少路/你才會稱他為男子漢？/一隻白鴿要在海上飛行多遠/才能在沙地上安眠？）

■ 歌詞中連問了兩個問題，都是以疑問副詞 how 為開頭的問句，這些問題是所謂的修辭上的問題，不見得需要答案。

「Extra Bonus」

■ 這首歌曲所問的問題，其實答案不言自明，就像飄過的風一般: The answer is blowing in the wind.

「HOW」

■ 疑問詞中最常讓人分不清楚的是 what 和 which，譬如，當我們問某人喜歡什麼運動時，通常會說 What sport do you like?而不是 Which sport do you like?

■ 問人喜歡什麼電影時，也是說 What kind of movies do you like?而不是 Which kind of movies do you like?基本上，用 what 來表示什麼樣的或哪一種時，範圍很廣泛，沒有特別指哪些項目，用 which 來表示類似的意思時，就是指某些項目中的哪一個。兩者有時可以相互替換，有時候不可以，像是上面所舉的幾個例子。

「Extra Bonus」

■ 舉例來說，在餐廳中當服務員問你喜歡哪中冰淇淋時，用 Which/what flavor of ice cream do you like?都可以? 因為眼前顯然有幾種選項讓你來選，此時用 which 更為恰當。

31-2 考試一點靈

文 法加油站

■ 疑問詞有時候面要接介系詞才能意義完整,這個介系詞不能省。

・Who did you go to the library with?

■ 這種介系詞也可以放到句首,但疑問代名詞要從主格的 who 改成受格的 whom。

・With whom did you go to the library?

■ 一般而言,受格的 whom 不會出現在句首,改由 who 代替,只有和介系詞一起出現時 whom 才會擺在句首。

・Who are you waiting for?/For whom are you waiting?

實 戰句

❶ No one has been able to fully explain an age-old question: What is time? Everyone knows-----time is. We can feel it. We have a sense of time. We know the difference between past, present, and future. But how does our sense of time relate to our perception of the outside world?

(A) how

(B) where

(C) what

(D) whose

中譯

沒有人能完全解釋一個古老的問題: 什麼是時間? 每個人都知道時間是什麼。我們能感受到時間，有時間感，知道過去、現在、和未來之間的差別。但我們的時間感如何與我們對外在世界的認知連接起來?

考題最前端

這題除了有直接問句，也有間接問句。What is time?是直接問句，可以獨立存在。what time is 是間接問句，必須以名詞子句形式存在於主要子句之中。how, where, what, whose 這幾個疑問詞都可帶出間接問句，但這裡只有 what 才符合句意，其他明顯不合。所以答案是 C。

答案：(C)

261

文 法加油站

■ 疑問句還有一種間接問句，是在句子中當成名詞子句之用，雖然有疑問句的形式，卻要用直述句的詞序。

- I don't know when he will come.（不能說成 I don't know when will he come.）

■ 疑問句中如果有間接問句，間接問句還是要用直述句的詞序。

- Can you tell me when he will come?

■ 間接問句也可以作為主詞。

- Who that man is remains a mystery to all.

實 戰句

❷ **Why do we age and is-----any way to slow aging? All people, especially women, want to know the secret to a longer life. Studies found that swapping out processed red meat like sausage for plant proteins was linked to a lower mortality rate.**

(A) why

(B) how

(C) what

(D) there

中譯

我們為何會衰老及是否有延緩老化的方法？所有的人，特別是女性，想要知道延長壽命的秘訣。研究顯示用植物性蛋白取代加工過的紅肉，和較低的死亡率有關連性。

考題最前端

這裡的第一個句子包含了兩個問題，一個是 Why do we age?另一個是 Is there any way to slow aging?由於這兩個問題相互關聯，所以可以放在同一個句子，初學者如果沒有把握，還是分兩個問句來問會比較保險。Is there 是 there is 句型的疑問句形式，如果是複數，則用 Are there。答案是 D。

答案：(D)

UNIT
32

熟悉序數

單 元概述

何謂序數？有何作用？

英文裡的數分為「數詞」（又稱基數）和「序數」，前者是 *one, two, three, four*…，後者則是 *first, second, third, fourth*…，表達出一種順序。序數的用途很廣，最常見的就是日期，還有樓層。序數之前要加上定冠詞 *the*，像是 *the first, the second, the third*…，但如果作為副詞，則不用加 *the*，像是 *He came here first.*

32-1 文法修行 **Let's Go**

Q32 請問你都怎麼記憶序數？有什麼更快的學習方式嗎？

Part
I
基礎實力養成篇

Part
II
進階文法修練篇

「**HOW**」

■ 每個基數都有相對應的序數，如 one/first, two/second, three/third, four/fourth, five/fifth 等，序數之所以必要，因為英文的日期表達一定會用到。譬如，9 月 1 日在書寫時只寫數詞 Sept. 1，唸的時候要唸成 September first，這個時候就非用到序數不可。

■ 基數變為序數有一定的規則，除了 first, second, third 外，其他許多都是在字尾加入 th，像是 fourth, sixth, seventh, eighth，five 的序數是 fifth，因為字尾是 ve，必須把 ve 改成 f，twelve 的序數是 twelfth。其他的變化還有去字尾 e 再加上 th（如 ninth），字尾是 ty 則把 ty 改成 tie，再加上 th（如 thirtieth）。

「**Extra Bonus**」

■ 如果碰到兩位數整數，只需改個位數為序數，如 twenty-five 改成 twenty-fifth。

「**HOW**」

■ 加拿大歌手麥可·布雷（Michael Buble）在他著名的歌曲〈為我留最後一支舞〉（Save The Last Dance For Me）中唱到: But while we're apart/Don't give your heart/To anyone/And don't forget who's taking you home/And in who's arms you're gonna be/So darling, save the last dance for me（然當我們分開/不要把妳的心/給任何人/且不要忘了誰將帶妳回家/妳將躺在誰的懷裡/所以達令，為我留最後一支舞）。

■ the last dance 字面上的意思是最後一支舞，但這只是一種比喻性的說法。

「**Extra Bonus**」

■ 如果 last 後面加上數字，可能會有不同的解釋，如 the last two days 可以表示過去兩天，也可能指最後兩天，此時就要看上下文而定。

「HOW」

■ 英文裡有一些用到序數的慣用語，如 the eleventh hour（最後一刻），the sixth sense（第六感），to the ninth degree（極度地，無窮地），the fourth estate（第四階級，通常指媒體），the seventh heaven（七重天，極樂世界），the third wheel（電燈泡，多餘的），the twelfth of never（永遠不會來到的日期），third time lucky（第三次嘗試可望成功），second best（次好的），first come first served（先來優先服務），the third world（第三世界，與其相對有第一世界 the first world 和第二世界 the second world）。

「Extra Bonus」

■ 序數也能構成動詞，如 second-guess（事後評論）

· Some political analysts are famous for second-guessing.

32-2 考試一點靈

文 法加油站

■ 序數之前除了加定冠詞 the，還可以加所有格，但所有格和定冠詞絕對不可以連用。

· Peter bought his second car.

■ 如果序數和數詞同時出現在名詞之前，序數在前、數詞在後。

· The first five customers will get a discount.

■ 序數當副詞時，要省略定冠詞 the 或所有格。

· He finished second in the race.

實 戰句

❶ The first-----dinosaur brain fossil was discovered on a British beach in 2004 as a fossil lump found on that beach was proven to contain mineralized tissue from a dinosaur's brain. The fossil belongs to genus of dinosaur related to Iguanodon, a herbivorous dinosaur that lived during the early Cretaceous.

(A) know

(B) known

(C) knew

(D) knows

中譯

　　第一個已知的恐龍腦部化石於 2004 年在英國的一處海灘被人發現，那個化石塊被證明含有礦石化的恐龍腦部組織。該化石屬於與禽龍屬相關的恐龍，那是一種生活在白堊紀初期的草食性恐龍。

考題最前端

　　前面提過名詞前面如果有序數和數詞或形容詞，詞序是序數在前，數詞或形容詞在後，這裡的 the first known dinosaur brain fossil 意思是第一個已知的恐龍腦部化石，也就是人類發現的第一個恐龍腦部化石。類似的説法還有 the first known analogue computer（第一個已知的類比式電腦），the first known computer virus（第一個已知的電腦病毒）。

答案：(B)

文 ▶ 法加油站

■ 英國王室的名稱在書寫上是在人名後面加上羅馬數字，可是唸的時候要唸成序數。

- Charles II—Charles the Second

■ once 也是序數，但通常用作頻率副詞。

- They see each other once every two weeks.

■ 用到 once 的慣用語很多，像是 once in a lifetime, once upon a time, once and for all。

- This is an once-in-a-lifetime chance.

實 戰句

❷ **As we know, China is now the world's-----largest economy after the U.S. However, China had been the world's largest economy in early 19th century as the Qing dynasty held the largest share of global gross domestic product (GDP).**

(A) two

(B) once

(C) second

(D) first

中譯

　　如我們所知，中國現在是僅次於美國的世界第二大經濟體。然而，中國在 19 世紀初期曾經是世界最大的經濟體，當時清朝的國內生產總值佔全世界最大的比例。

考題最前端

　　這題仍然在測驗考生對序數詞序的熟悉度，不管序數後面有什麼形容詞，它總是擺在第一個位置，如 second largest, third largest, fourth largest，或是 first few customers, last few days。不過要注意，所有格或定冠詞的位置要在序數之前，如 the world's second largest economy，his second car，但所有格和定冠詞不能同時出現。所以答案是 C。

答案：(C)

認識比較級和最高級

單 元概述

何謂比較級和最高級？兩者之間的差異為何？

形容詞為了表達不同層級的意義，會在字形或用法上發生變化，於是產生了比較級和最高級形容詞，比較級是比較兩個人或物，表示其中一個「比較…」，而最高級是比較三個或三個以上的人或物，表示其中一個「最…」。比較級要和連接詞 than 一起用，而最高級通常後面接介系詞 in，表示在某個團體或群組裡的最高狀態，但不一定要和 in 搭配使用。

33-1 文法修行 Let's Go

Q33 請問你都怎麼記憶比較級和最高級？有什麼更快的學習方式嗎？

「HOW」

■ 比較級和最高級形容詞比較麻煩的地方就是字形的變化。一般而言，比較級要在形容詞字尾加上 er，最高級則是在字尾加上 est，但前提是要單音節的形容詞才行。例如 dark, long, kind 這類的規則變化，dark/darker/darkest，long/longer/longest，kind/kinder/kindest。

■ 如果碰上兩個音節或兩個音節以上的形容詞，其比較級和最高級的變化就是在字尾加上 more（比較級）和 most（最高級），或是表示較少的 less 和最少的 least。但多音節形容詞如果字尾是 y，其比較級和最高級是要去掉 y 改成 ier 和 iest，如 dirty/dirtier/dirtiest。

「Extra Bonus」

■ 規則變化的比較級和最高級形容詞比較好懂，真正麻煩的是不規則變化的比較級和最高級，這些留待稍後介紹。

「HOW」

■ 美國歌手凱莉‧克拉克森（Kelly Clarkson）有一首歌叫做〈更堅強〉（Stronger），歌詞有這段文詞:What doesn't kill you makes you stronger/ Stand a little taller/Doesn't mean I'm lonely when I'm alone/What doesn't kill you makes you a fighter（殺不死你的東西將使你變得更堅強/站得更高一點/我獨自一人不代表我孤單/殺不死你的東西將使你成為一個戰士）

■ stronger 是 strong 的比較級，使役動詞 make 接受詞再接形容詞或過去分詞，比較級也是形容詞的一種。用 makes you become stronger 這個說法也行，但比較不簡潔。

「Extra Bonus」

■ 比較級一般後面要接連接詞 than，但也可以不接，只要句意清楚就行。Stand a little taller. 後面可以接 than before 或 than you used to，但加不加都不會影響句意的完整。

「HOW」

■ 比較級和最高級形容詞的不規則變化要靠記憶才行，因為和原來的形容詞原級完全地不同。

■ 譬如，good 和 well 的比較級和最高級是 better 和 best; bad 和 ill 則變化成 worse 和 worst; far 有兩種變化，一個是 farther 和 farthest（指距離和空間上的遠）。

■ 另一個是 further 和 furthest（指時間、程度、數量上的差距）; few 是 fewer 和 fewest; little 是 less 和 least; many 和 much 都是 more 和 most。這些不規則變化是最常見的，平時多注意應該就可以在考試時不會搞混。

「Extra Bonus」

■ farther 純粹指距離，further 則主要表達程度。
- For further information, please call the information center.（這裡就不能用 farther）。

275

33-2 考試一點靈

文 法加油站

■ 比較級是兩者之間的比較，要用到連接詞 than。

· Mr. Lin is older than Mr. Chen.

■ 比較級前面可以加倍數詞（two times, three times 等）來表示倍數。

· My house is three times bigger than yours.（也可以說成 My house is three times as big as yours.）

■ 比較級前面可以加 much/far/any/no/rather/a little/even 等副詞來修飾。

· This idea is much better than that one.

實 戰句

❶ **The federal spending of the U.S. is divided into three categories: mandatory spending, discretionary spending and interest on debt. The first two categories account for more than 90 percent of all federal spending. Interest on debt is a much-----amount than the other two categories.**

(A) small

(B) smallest

(C) more small

(D) smaller

中譯

美國的聯邦預算分為三類: 強制性支出、自由裁量支出、及債務利息。前兩種佔聯邦預算的 90%以上，債務利息所佔的比例要比其他兩種小了很多。

考題最前端

比較級前面可以加 much 或 far 等副詞來修飾，表示更高一級，但還沒到最高級。所以比較級中也是有程度之分，要用 much 之類副詞來加以強化。The first two categories account for more than 90 percent of all federal spending.可以改成 The first two categories account for the greatest portion of the federal spending. 剛好符合這個單元所介紹的最高級。

答案：(D)

文 法加油站

■ 最高級形容詞後面通常接介系詞 in 或 of，in 表示在一個地方或團體之中，of 表示在一群人之中。

· Rick is the tallest of basketball players in his school./Rick is the tallest Basketball player in his school.

■ 有時可以用 among 代替 of。

· Charles is the most intelligent among/of the boys.

■ 最高級有時不見得表達最高等級，而是一種修辭上的稱讚，像是常聽到的 one of the best，最好的通常只有一個，但外國人很少說什麼是 the best，只會說 one of the best。

· Taipei is one of the best cities I have ever visited.

實 戰句

❷ **The discovery of blood circulation, one of the----- important discoveries in medicine, is credited to the English physician William Harvey. Harvey focused much of his research on blood flow in the human body. Most physicians of the time assumed that the lungs were responsible for blood circulation.**

(A) better

(B) most

(C) best

(D) mostly

中譯

　　血液流動的發現是醫學上最重要的發現之一，這要歸功於英國醫師威廉·哈維。哈維花了許多功夫在研究人體的血液流動，與他同一時期的醫師大多認為肺才是負責血液的流動。

考題最前端

　　以英語為母語的人通常不會直接稱某人或某事為 the best 或 the most important，而是用 one of the best 或 one of the most important 來表達其重要性。客觀上來說，沒有任何人或事能稱得上最好或最重要，除非是求學階段可以用成績來衡量的那種。既然是 one of the most important，就表示有好幾樣，所以 important 後面要用複數名詞 discoveries。答案是 B。

答案：(B)

UNIT 34 認識從屬連接詞

單 元概述

何謂從屬連接詞？有何功能？

從屬連接詞引導從屬子句，這些從屬子句如果是名詞字句或形容詞子句，通常存在於主要子句之中，如果是副詞子句，則用從屬連接詞把副詞子句與主要子句分開來。不管是哪一種附屬子句，都無法單獨存在，都必須和主要子句連在一起有意義。

34-1 文法修行 Let's Go

Q34 請問你都怎麼記憶從屬連接詞？有什麼更快的學習方式嗎？

「HOW」

■ 從屬連接詞很多，有 after, ever since, that, although, if, as, unless, as long as, until, once, when, because, before, since, so that 等，大部分都是引導副詞子句，that 則最常被用來帶出名詞子句，需要特別介紹一下。that 引導的名詞子句最常見的是在動詞後面出現的那種，例如：I think that she is very smart. 這是直接放在動詞後面，也有在受詞後面，例如：She told me that she made a mistake.像是直接受詞和間接受詞的用法。另一種 that 子句是放在形容詞後面，例如： I am sure that we will succeed.

「Extra Bonus」

■ 後面可以接 that 子句的形容詞通常是表示感情或心理之類的形容詞，像是 sure, glad, sorry, disappointed。這類句型可以省略 that。

· He was disappointed（that）he was not invited to the party.

「HOW」

■ 美國鄉村歌手比爾·安德森（Bill Anderson）有一首歌叫做〈依然〉（Still），其中有這段歌詞：Still/though you broke my heart/Still/though we're far apart/I love you still（依然/雖然妳傷了我的心/雖然我們相隔遙遠/我依然愛妳）

■ though 就是一個從屬連接詞，基本上和 although 的意思差不多，也可以相互替換，但口語上似乎有偏愛用 though 的趨向，尤其是 though 前面還可以加 even 來加強語氣，although 卻不行。Though you broke my heart, I love you still.這句話前面是過去式，後面是現在式，因為傷了心是過去發生的，而愛意仍持續到現在。

「Extra Bonus」

■ still 也可以作為從屬連接詞，只是比較少人知道。意思是然而、但是、儘管如此。

· She is very attractive, still I don't like her.

「HOW」

■ 從屬連接詞大部分都在引導副詞子句，像是 before, after, though, although, because, till, until, if, unless 等。副詞子句不能單獨存在，因為其功能是在修飾主要子句，所以才稱副詞子句。

■ 可是 before 和 after 本身也可以是介系詞，如何區分它們什麼時候是從屬連接詞，什麼時候是介系詞？其實很簡單，只要 before 和 after 後面跟的是一個完整的子句，就是從屬連接詞，如果後面跟的是片語，那就是介系詞，例如：He took a walk after he finished his work. 裡面的 after 是連接詞，He took a walk after dinner. 這裡的 after 是介系詞。

「Extra Bonus」

■ 副詞子句的作用類似副詞，就算去掉也不影響主要子句的文法完整性，但句意會顯得不完整。

· He took a walk. 是一個完整的句子，但加上 after he finished his work 這個附屬子句就意思就變得比較豐富。

34-2 考試一點靈

文 法加油站

■ that 所引導的子句不但可以放在動詞和述詞形容詞後面，還能放在句首作為主詞，此時其性質為名詞子句。

· That the world is changing faster and faster seems to be true.

■ 疑問詞所引導的子句也可以放在動詞後面作為名詞子句。

· I do not know when they will arrive.

■ whether 和 that 一樣可以引導名詞子句作為主詞、受詞、或補語，作為主詞不能和 if 相互替換，其他狀況可以。

· Whether he will support us（or not）is very important.（此時不能用 if 代替 whether）

實 戰句

❶ -----many future transportation systems depend on higher power density and more efficient compact motors, conventional materials and technologies cannot meet the demand. The development of higher-temperature superconducting materials is considered to offer a solution.

(A) Though

(B) Whether

(C) As

(D) Unless

中譯

　　隨著許多未來運輸系統要靠更高電力強度和更有效率的小型馬達，傳統的材料和科技已經無法滿足需求。較高溫超導體的開發被視為可以提供解決方案。

考題最前端

　　作為從屬連接詞，as 有好幾個意思: 當…時、隨著、因為、雖然。這裡的 as 可以解釋為當…時、隨著、或因為，不管哪個意思，都是在引導一個從屬的副詞子句，目的是修飾後面的主要子句。as 用來表達原因時，其原因通常是已知、不用特別解釋的，此時可以用 since 來替換。答案是 C。

答案：(C)

文 ▶ 法加油站

■ 關係代名詞（who, whom, that, which, whose）也具有連接詞的功
能，所引導的子句是形容詞子句，無法獨立存在，必須依附在主要子
句才行。

　　· People who love to laugh at others are not respectable.

■ 從屬連接詞中有一種是由分開的兩個字組成，亦即 so…that 和 such…
that，這兩個意思完全一樣，只不過 so 後面要接形容詞，such 後面要
接冠詞和名詞。

　　· The book was so boring that I fell asleep while reading it./It was
　　　such a boring book that I fell asleep while reading it.

■ 另一個類似的從屬連接詞是 so that 和 in order that，它們的意思不是
太怎麼樣而怎麼樣，而是為了什麼目的。記住，so that 和 in order
that 不可以像 so…that 一樣分開來。

　　· He works hard so that he can earn enough money to buy a house.

實 戰句

❷ -----a trip to Mars may not be possible in the near future, more than 78,000 people have applied to a program launched by a Dutch company, which solicits volunteers to be trained as astronauts for a one-way trip to the red planet.

(A) Despite

(B) Though

(C) If

(D) Whether

中譯

　　雖然近期之內火星之旅或許還不可能，7 萬 8000 多人卻向一家荷蘭公司提出申請，志願接受該公司培訓，成為單程紅色星球之旅的太空人。

考題最前端

　　這題的答案用 although 也可以，不過選項中不可能同時提供 though 和 although，這樣就成了複選題。之前提過，though 的使用頻率有越來越增加的趨勢，尤其是在口語或非正式的文章中。despite 也表達類似的意思，但它是介系詞，後面不能接一個完整的子句，只能接片語，如果改成 despite the fact that 就可以接一個子句。答案是 B。

答案：(B)

UNIT 35 介系詞的用法

單 元概述

何謂介系詞？有何功能？

介系詞是一種放在名詞、名詞片語、或代名詞之前，用來與另一個字連結的字，例如: *I prefer to read in the library.* 句子裡的 *in* 就是介系詞，後面接定冠詞 *the* 和名詞 *library*，構成一個介系詞片語，用來修飾動詞 *read*，表示地點。英文的介系詞有 *100* 以上，但常用的就幾十個，像是 *on, at, about, in, between, behind, under, before, after* 等。

35-1 文法修行 Let's Go

Q35 請問你都怎麼記憶介系詞？有什麼更快的學習方式嗎？

「HOW」

■ 介系詞後面一定要有受詞，受詞有好幾種：名詞、代名詞、動名詞、名詞子句。如果接名詞，記得有時候名詞前面還要加定冠詞 the。例如：Meet me at the train station.如果接代名詞，要用受格代名詞：I went to see a movie with her.

■ 如果接動名詞，動名詞後面可能還要接介系詞或受詞: My friend used my motorcycle without asking for my permission.如果是名詞子句，通常是 whether 所引導的名詞子句: The final decision depends on whether they can reach an agreement.

「Extra Bonus」

■ 介系詞也有複合介系詞，也就是由兩個以上介系詞所構成。像是 in front of, in case of, in spite, along with, because of, instead of。

「HOW」

■ 美國歌手威利·尼爾森（Willie Nelson）有一首經典的歌曲〈總是在我心上〉（Always On My Mind），歌詞中有這段: If I made you feel second best/Girl, I'm sorry I was blind/But you were always on my mind/You were always on my mind（如果我讓妳覺得只是次好/丫頭，抱歉是我瞎了眼/但妳總是在我心上/妳總是在我心上）

■ on one's mind 是一個慣用語，意思是想念著，與其類似的是 in one's mind，但意思是看法或想法，和 on one's mind 不一樣。

「Extra Bonus」

■ 類似的慣用語還有 in one's heart，意思是內心深處。
· She knows in her heart that they did the right thing.

「HOW」

■ 介系詞的種類有：表示時間的介系詞（at, on, in, for, since, during, through, from…to, until, by）、表示地點的介系詞（in, at, on, by, against, near）、表示位置的介系詞（at, on, in, above, over, below, under, behind, in front of, before）、表示移動方向的介系詞（to, forward）。

■ 在這些介系詞當中，at, in, on 是最常出現的，既可以表達時間，也能表達地點。簡單來說，at 所表達的範圍比較小，on 的範圍比較大，in 則涵蓋最大的範圍。例如，at 表達時間時是指幾點，on 是指哪一天，in 則是指哪一年。

「Extra Bonus」

■ 雖說 in 指的是比較大的範圍，像是 in Asia, in America, in Africa，但是說到在什麼大陸時，卻要用 on the continent。

· On the continent of Africa, many animals are on the verge of extinction because of poaching.

35-2 考試一點靈

文 法加油站

■ 有些慣用語是介系詞後加形容詞，看起來不合文法，卻是約定俗成的說法。像是 for free, for sure, for certain
  - I can't say for certain when he will come.

■ 有些慣用語如 from abroad 或 from outside，看起來像是介系詞後面加副詞，其實 abroad 和 outside 也可以當成名詞，作為介系詞的受詞。
  - Visitors from abroad are increasing.

■ 慣用語也有出現連續兩個介系詞，如 from under your nose。
  - She stole a book from under the bookstore clerk's nose.

實 戰句

❶ -----the world's largest producer of nuclear power, the U.S. has 100 nuclear reactors producing 805 billion kWh in 2016. There are two reactors under construction. But construction of the two reactors was halted on July 31, 2017 because of increasing costs and repeated building delays.

(A) Of

(B) In

(C) Among

(D) As

中譯

　　作為世界最大的核能生產國，美國 2016 年有 100 座核子反應爐，總共生產了 8050 億度電。現在有兩座正在興建當中。但這兩座的興建工作於 2017 年 7 月 31 日暫停，原因是費用的增加和不斷的施工延遲。

考題最前端

　　上一個單元介紹了作為從屬連接詞的 as，到了本單元，as 搖身一變成了介系詞，所以說它的功用真的很大，像是一個工具人。作為介系詞時，as 的意思是作為、以…的身分、當作、像、如同。這裡的意思是作為，表示美國是世界最大的核能生產國。As the world's largest producer of nuclear power 也可以寫成 Being the world's largest producer of nuclear power，這是分詞構句，留待稍後的單元再介紹。答案是 D。

答案：(D)

文 法加油站

■ 有時聽到有人說 in school，也有人說 at school，其實兩者都對，前者是美式英語的說法，後者是英式英語的說法。但前者比較強調上學（中小學），指還在念書，後者指在學校裡。

- Children were not at school yesterday, because yesterday was a holiday.

■ 另一常用的介系詞是 of，它的用處很廣，除了放在兩個名詞（前面通常為數詞）之間表示所屬關係，還可以表達原因或材料。

Two of the players got injured in the game.

■ 表示原因時，of 是指直接原因，from 則表示間接原因。

- Mr. Chen died of cancer./Many people in underdeveloped countries die from poverty.

實 戰句

❷ The situation-----the Korean Peninsula has tensed up because of North Korea's repeated missile and nuclear tests, arousing condemnation from around the world. China, North Korea's long-term ally, joins other countries in condemning the missile and nuclear tests.

(A) in
(B) on
(C) at
(D) over

中譯

　　朝鮮半島情勢因北韓不斷的飛彈試射和核子試驗而緊張起來，引發全世界的譴責。北韓的長期盟友中國也加入其他國家共同譴責這些飛彈試射和核子試驗。

考題最前端

　　之前提過大的地方要用 in，像是 in Africa, in China 等，可是有些大範圍地域卻要用 on，像是 peninsula 和 continent，同學會問為什麼？語言是約定俗成，而且規則之外總有例外，特別注意一下就好。from around the world 是另一個會引起困惑的說法，因為用到了兩個介系詞，只能說這是現在很受歡迎的說法，雖然文法上有點說不過去。

答案：(B)

熟悉介系詞片語

單 元概述

何謂介系詞片語？有何作用？

介系詞片語是由介系詞所開頭的片語，介系詞後面要接名詞或代名詞，兩者之間通常會有冠詞或所有格之類的修飾語。介系詞後面也能接動名詞或子句，兩者之間通常不需要修飾語。介系詞片語有三個主要功能：當名詞用，作為句子的主詞或補語；當形容詞用，修飾名詞或作為補語；當副詞用，修飾動詞、形容詞、其他副詞或整個句子。

36-1 文法修行 Let's Go

Q36 請問你都怎麼記憶介系詞片語？有什麼更快的學習方式嗎？

「HOW」

　　介系詞片語的最基本形式就是介系詞加名詞、代名詞（受格）、動名詞、或子句，例如：at home, in time, with us, by cheating, from my mother, about what customers need。比較長的如：under the sky, in the garden, along the way, with or without you, on the floor 介系詞片語常常放在名詞後面作為形容詞片語，例如：The toy on the kitchen floor is to be discarded.介系詞片語 on the kitchen floor 是在修飾 toy，如果不清楚為什麼有這樣的句型，可以把句子改成 The toy which is on the floor is to be discarded. 之前介紹過形容詞子句在關係代名詞為主格時可以省略關係代名詞及關係子句中的動詞，剩下來的就成為一個介系詞片語。

「Extra Bonus」

■ 同樣是 on the floor，位置相同不見得功能也一樣。

・When you drop a book on the floor, it will create a loud noise.（這裡的 on the floor 就成了修飾動詞 drop 的副詞片語，而不是修飾 book 的形容詞片語）

「HOW」

■ 美國歌手保羅‧賽門（Paul Simon）在他知名的歌曲〈惡水上的橋〉（Bridge Over Trouble Water）中唱到：When times get rough/And friends just can't be found/Like a bridge over troubled water/I will lay me down（當時機惡劣/又找不到朋友時/像一座惡水上的橋/我將趴伏下來）

■ 這首歌很感人，有點像中文裡願為朋友兩肋插刀的意思，a bridge over troubles water 中的 over troubled water 就是介系詞片語，用來修飾前面的 bridge。lay me down 中的 lay down 是片語動詞，也就是動詞和介系詞結合在一起的慣用語。

「Extra Bonus」

■ 這首歌的歌詞還有另一句話也用到介系詞片語，即 in your eyes。

  ‧ When tears are in your eyes, I will dry them all.

「HOW」

■ 介系詞片語不會影響到所修飾名詞或代名詞（如果是句子的主詞）的動詞單複數，這一點很容易讓人搞錯。例如: Neither of these books contains the information I need.句子裡的主詞是代名詞 neither，of these books 是修飾它的介系詞片語，很多人看到 these books 就自然以為是一個複數的主詞，其實是錯的。

■ either 也是：Either of the students is intelligent enough to teach other students.這裡的 of the students 也是介系詞片語，用來修飾主詞 either。同樣地，主詞是 one of them 時，動詞也應該單數動詞。

「Extra Bonus」

■ 類似的例子還有 none，不過現在也有人主張它後面接單複數動詞皆可。

· None of the machines is/are working.

36-2 考試一點靈

文 法加油站

■ 有些介系詞，像是 along with 和 in addition to，出現在主詞後面會讓人誤以為又連接了一個主詞，事實上主詞只有前面那一個。

・ Tom, along with other students, plans to go swimming.

■ 介系詞片語部分可以作為副詞片語，通常放在句首或句尾。

・ Every day after breakfast, the old man takes a walk in the park.

■ 介系詞片語可以作為副詞片語，可是副詞片語還包含其他片語，像是不定詞片語。

・ Every day after dinner, Peter goes to a nearby convenience store to buy a cup of coffee.（after dinner 是介系詞片語，作為副詞之用，to a nearby convenience store 也是介系詞片語，是修飾動詞 goes 的副詞片語，而 to buy a cup of coffee 則是表達目的的不定詞片語，也是副詞片語。）

實 戰句

❶ **The luxury market is headed toward customization or personalization as mass-produced items are no longer that popular because of their uniformity. Mass**

production is aimed at keeping costs down, which requires items-----the assembly line to be largely identical.

(A) in

(B) at

(C) on

(D) to

中譯

奢侈品市場朝向客製化或個人化的方向邁進，大量製造的產品由於看起來都一樣已不再那麼受歡迎。量產的目的是為了降低成本，這就需要讓裝配線上的產品大致上一致。

考題最前端

之前提過在朝鮮半島要用 on the Korean Peninsula，為何用 on 而不是 in？語言本來就是約定俗成，有時不能用單一的規則加以律定。在生產線上的英文是 on the assembly line，介系詞要用 on。有趣的是，排隊的英文是 stand in line，而不是 stand on line。同樣的，我們在同一個隊伍裡，英文是 We are on the same team.而不是 We are in the same team. 答案是 C。

答案：(C)

■ 介系詞片語最常用 in 來表示一段時間，像是 in a few days, in a few years。

  ・He will be back in a few days.（此時 in a few days 是副詞片語）

■ to 則是用來表達地點。

  ・We will drive to Taipei tomorrow.（to Taipei 是一個作為副詞的介系詞片語）

■ 有些形容詞後面要接介系詞片語才能表達意思，像是 sorry。

  ・I feel sorry for your loss.

實 戰句

❷ **Taipei 101, an iconic skyscraper in Taipei, is prone to earthquakes and fierce winds. That's why it has a gigantic tuned mass damper suspended from the 92nd to the 87th floor. The damper, acting-----a pendulum, helps the building maintain stability during strong gusts of wind.**

(A) in

(B) like

(C) on

(D) at

中譯

　　作為台北市的代表性摩天大樓，台北 101 容易受到地震和強風的影響。那是它在 87 至 92 樓間裝了一個巨大的阻尼器的原因。阻尼器像鐘擺一樣發揮作用，協助讓整棟建築在強陣風時維持穩定。

考題最前端

　　這題包含好幾個介系詞片語: from the 92nd to the 87th floor, like a pendulum, during strong gusts of wind。這些介系詞片語都是副詞片語，功能在於修飾動詞。like a pendulum 修飾動詞 act，這個動詞本來是形容詞子句中的動詞，因為把形容詞子句簡化後只剩分詞形式，原來的樣子是這樣: The damper, which acts like a pendulum, helps…。答案是 B。

答案：(B)

UNIT
37

了解片語動詞

單 元概述

何謂片語動詞？有何功能？

片語動詞不是動詞片語，它是由動詞後面加上介系詞或副詞構成，意義和原來的動詞不同。片語動詞應該被當一個由多個字構成的動詞，也稱為多字動詞，可分為及物和不及物。常見的不及物片語動詞有 *get up*，後面不必接受詞。常見的及物片語動詞有 *put off*，後面要接受詞，才能表達出延後了什麼。

37-1 文法修行 Let's Go

Q37 請問你都怎麼記憶片語動詞？有什麼更快的學習方式嗎？

「HOW」

■ 片語動詞有 1000 個以上，但常用的有 200 多個，要稍微下點功夫才能搞熟。片語動詞有些可以分開，有些則不能分開。先來看不可分開的：blow up, break down, break in, break up, call on, catch up, check in, check out, come from, count on, do away with, eat out, end up, fall apart, get away with, get together, get up, give in, go after, go ahead, go out, grow out of, hang on, hang out, hold on, log in, log out, look after, look forward to, pass away, put up with, run into, take after, take off, warm up, work out 等。這些有的是及物，有的是不及物，與其記哪些是及物哪些是不及物，還不如弄清楚哪些可以分開那些不可以分開。

「Extra Bonus」

■ 關鍵在於搞動可分開和不可分開的片語動詞，搞清楚哪些片語動詞是不可以分開後，就比較不會出錯。

• You look after someone. 而不是 You look someone after.

「HOW」

■ 美國老牌的木匠兄妹合唱團（the Carpenters）在他們膾炙人口的歌曲〈世界之頂〉（Top of The World）中唱到：Such a feelin's comin' over me/There is wonder in most everything I see/Not a cloud in the sky/Got the sun in my eyes/And I won't be surprised if it's a dream（這樣一種感覺迎面而來/我對看到的事物大多感到驚奇/天空中沒有任何的雲/眼睛看出去的都是陽光/如果這一切都是個夢，我一點也不會驚訝）

■ come over 是一個片語動詞，意思是突然間對某人產生強烈的影響。它顯然是及物片語動詞，且不可以分開，不能寫成 come me over。

「Extra Bonus」

■ 歌詞中還有另一個片語動詞 look down on，意思是往下看，但它也有另一個意思，即輕視。

· I'm on the top of the world looking down on creation.（這裡就是往下看的意思）

「HOW」

■ 不可分開的片語動詞比較好記，使用上也比較不會出錯，但看起來比較單調，所以可分開的片語動詞就有其必要。片語動物要及物才能接受詞，而這個受詞就可以彈性地擺在片語動詞的中間或後面，但如果受詞為代名詞，就只能放在片語動詞的後面，這很重要，一定要記住。

■ 例如：They turned down my proposal./They turned my proposal down.這兩種寫法都可以，因為受詞是名詞 proposal，前面的 my 是修飾語; We saw her off at the airport.（寫成 We saw off her at the airport.就不對，因為受詞是代名詞 her）

「Extra Bonus」

■ 類似的例子很多，像是 give back the money/give the money back, knock over the glass/knock the glass over。
  - She gave it back.和 He knocked it over.（受詞是代名詞時只能放在中間）

307

37-2 考試一點靈

文 法加油站

■ 以 ly 結尾的情態副詞，不可以放在不及物片語動詞的中間，只能在後面。

- He gave up quickly.（不能寫成 He gave quickly up）

■ 情態副詞不可位於及物片語動詞與其受詞之間。

- He put out the fire quickly.（不能寫成 He put out quickly the fire.）

■ 在關係子句和疑問句中，及物片語動詞基本上不可分開。

- The company that he took over is heavily in debt.

實 戰句

❶ **Cassini, the first spacecraft to orbit Saturn, has allowed people on earth to have an in-depth study of the second largest planet in the Solar System. As executing the first of five ultra-close passes of the Saturn, the satellite passed-----its upper atmosphere, promising new data on the chemical composition of the planet.**

(A) away

(B) off

(C) through

(D) among

中譯

　　第一個繞行土星的太空船卡西尼號讓地球上的人們可以深入研究太陽系的第二大行星。在對土星執行第一次超近距離繞行時，這個人造衛星通過土星的上層大氣層，有希望取得有關這個行星化學組成的新數據。

考題最前端

　　片語動詞 pass through 是經過的意思，pass away 和 pass off 也是由 pass 構成的片語動詞，但意思不符合，前者是指死亡，後者是進行、完成之意。並沒有 pass among 這樣的組合。這裡的 pass through 就不能分開，受詞 its upper atmosphere 一定要在 through 的後面。由 pass 組成的片語動詞至少有 16 個，其他還有 pass by, pass down, pass for, pass on to 等。

答案：(C)

文 法加油站

■ 部分及物片語動詞在關係子句和疑問句中可以分開。

· The paper that he worked on was completed./The paper on which he worked on was completed.

■ 部分及物片語動詞可以被動形式出現。

· Many employees of the company were laid off./The company laid off many employees.

■ 可以構成片語動詞的動詞主要有 bring（about, along, in, off, up）、call（off, up）、give（away, back）、push（about, around）、take（away, apart, back, down, off, over）、think（over, through）等。

· It was so hot that he took off his shirt.

實 戰句

❷ **A civilian landed his US$350 drone on the flight deck of HMS Queen Elizabeth, the United Kingdom's new aircraft carrier, without being noticed by anyone. The drone operator, a photographer, flew the drone----- Queen Elizabeth as she was docked at a port in Scotland.**

(A) over

(B) in

(C) between

(D) at

中譯

　　一位平民百姓把他一架價值 350 美元的無人機降落在英國最新的航空母艦伊莉莎白女王號上，居然沒有被人發現。這架無人機的操縱者是一個攝影師，他在伊莉莎白女王號停泊在蘇格蘭一個港口時把無人機從船的上空飛過。

考題最前端

　　片語動詞 fly over 是飛越的意思，本來是用人或飛機作主詞，但現在由於是無人機，必須由人操作，所以變成人 flew the drone over 航空母艦。由 fly 組成的片語動詞不算多，有的意思和 fly 完全沒有關係，如 fly at，意思是批評或咆哮。fly around 則是流傳的意思。fly into 表示很快的情緒變化，如 He flew into a rage.答案是 A。

答案：(A)

熟悉分詞構句

單 元概述

何謂分詞構句？有何功能？

分詞構句又稱分詞片語或分詞子句，具有形容詞子句或副詞子句的功能。分詞構句通常是由副詞子句或形容詞子句演變而來，也就是把原來的從屬子句簡化成片語形式。最常見的句型之一有：*Walking on the street, I met an old friend.* 原來的句子是 *When I walked on the street, I met an old friend.* 簡化副詞子句或其他類型從屬子句的原則是當兩個子句主詞相同，就去掉從屬子句的連接詞和主詞，將動詞改成分詞形式。

38-1 文法修行 Let's Go

Q38 請問你都怎麼記憶分詞構句？有什麼更快的學習方式嗎？

「HOW」

■ 分詞構句基本上就是把從屬子句簡化成片語，讓句子變得比較簡潔有力，不簡化也行，但看起來比較累贅。分詞構句可以放在句首（通常是從副詞子句改來）、句中（通常是改自形容詞子句）、句尾（通常表示同時進行的動作）。其中又以句首的分詞構句最為常見，也最常被用到。另外有一些經常用到的獨立分詞片語，它們真的就只是片語，不是簡化的從屬子句，通常放在句首作為一種起承轉合的用語，像是 generally speaking, strictly speaking, judging from, considering, given the condition 等。

「Extra Bonus」

■ 分詞構句不見得只有有現在分詞，也有過去分詞。

· Seen from a different perspective, the book becomes more interesting.（As it is seen from a different perspective, the book becomes more interesting.）

「HOW」

■ 英國樂團披頭四有一首叫做〈她正離開家〉（She's Leaving Home）的歌曲，其中有這一段: Wednesday morning at five o'clock as the day begins/Silently closing her bedroom door/Leaving the note that she hoped would say more/She goes down the stairs to the kitchen clutching her handkerchief（星期三早上五點天剛亮/輕輕地關上臥室的門/留下一張她希望可以表達更多的字條/她走下樓梯到廚房，手裡抓著手帕）

■ 歌詞裡用到好幾個分詞構句：silently closing⋯、leaving the note⋯、及 clutching her handkerchief，前面兩個是改自副詞子句，最後一個則是表示同時進行的動作。

「Extra Bonus」

■ 分詞構句在表達同時進行的動作時，最基本的型態就是動詞接分詞。

・He came running.（他跑著過來）

「HOW」

■ 分詞構句可以表示同時進行的事情、正在做什麼、動作的連續、原因和理由，平時不妨練習把分詞構句還原成原來的句型，就會比較了解分詞構句的意義。表示正在做什麼時，可以用從屬連接詞 when 或 while 來加以還原：Walking in the park, the old man found a stray dog.（When he was walking in the par, the old man found a stray dog.）

■ 表示原因和理由時，可以用連接詞 because, since, as 來加以還原：Living in a small town, Paul does not need a car.（Paul does not need a car since he lives in a small town.）

「Extra Bonus」

■ 當分詞構句表示連續的動作時，可以用對等連接詞 and 來還原原本需要兩個子句或動詞的句型。

· Wiping sweat from forehead, he reached for a bottle of water.（He wiped sweat from forehead and reached for a bottle of water.）

38-2 考試一點靈

文 法加油站

■ 分詞構句的否定形式是直接在分詞前面加 not 和 never。

  · Not knowing what to do, the suspect surrendered.

■ 分詞構句也有完成式，表示發生的時間早於主要子句的動詞。

  · Having searched relevant information on the Internet, the young couple knew what to order from the menu.（Because they had searched relevant information on the Internet, the young couple knew what to order from the menu.）

■ 有時分詞構句前面可以保留原本應該省略的從屬連接詞，像是 when 和 while。

  · While having a tour around Taipei, Mr. Smith tasted some of the best local foods.（也可以把 while 去掉，但保留 while 是為了強調那段期間）

實 戰句

❶ -----to 83 on average, the Japanese are the longest-living people in the world. The island of Okinawa, part of Japan, has the highest rate of centenarians. It is home to

a longevity research center. What's the secret to local people's longevity? Healthy diets and social activities are two key factors.

(A) Lived

(B) Having lived

(C) Living

(D) Lives

中譯

平均壽命達 83 歲的日本人是世界上最長壽的民族。日本所屬的沖繩島擁有最高比例的百歲人瑞,那裏設立了一個長壽研究中心。當地人民的長壽秘訣維何?健康的膳食和社交活動是兩個主要因素。

考題最前端

之前提過分詞構句可以表示原因或時間,但有時只是在描述一種狀態,像是這裡的 Living to 83 on average,把它放到 the Japanese 後面亦可: The Japanese, living to 83 on average, are the longest-living…. ,這種放在句中的分詞構句就是簡化成片語的形容詞子句,記得前後要用逗號來表達非限定用法。分詞構句可以靈活運用,擺在句首、句中、句尾皆可,但 living to 83 on average 這個例子只能放在句首和句中。答案是 C。

答案:(C)

317

- 分詞構句意義上的主詞如果和主要子句的主詞不同，必須在分詞構句用到 it 或 there 來加以區別。

  - It being a rainy day, I cancelled all the appointments.（Because it was a rainy day, I cancelled all the appointments.）

- 如果原來的句子是 there+be 動詞句型，改成分詞構句就必須保留 there be 的形式。

  - There being a shortage of supplies, they had to call for help.（Because there was a shortage of supplies, they had to call for help.）

- 分詞構句原本放在句首的，也可以放到主詞後面。

  - Henry, having finished his homework, started playing video games.（原本是 Having finished his homework, Henry started playing video games.）

實 戰句

❷ -----with rhesus macaque monkeys whose face recognition systems resemble humans', researchers at the Rockefeller University have begun to unravel how the brain recognizes familiar faces. They discovered two previously unknown areas of the brain that might help

explain the mechanisms underlying face recognition.

(A) Working

(B) Worked

(C) Work

(D) Having worked

中譯

　　洛克斐勒大學研究員研究臉部辨識系統類似人類的恆河猴後開始解開腦部如何辨識熟悉臉孔的奧秘。他們發現兩個之前未被人知曉的大腦區域，或許有助於解釋人臉辨識背後不為人知的機制。

考題最前端

　　這一題的分詞構句也是放在句首，表達研究人員的研究狀態，所以也可以放到主詞後面作為一種補充說明的分詞片語。這種句型很常見，尤其是學術文章中。後面還有一個分詞片語，即 underlying face recognition，它原來是個修飾 mechanisms 的形容詞子句: the mechanism that underlie face recognition，簡化之後就成了 the mechanisms underlying face recognition.答案是 A。

答案：(A)

Part I 基礎實力養成篇

Part II 進階文法修練篇

熟悉同位語

單 元概述

　　何謂同位語？有何功能？

　　同位語是用來說明或補充說明一個名詞的名詞或名詞片語，可以放在該名詞的前面或後面，通常要用逗號把兩者分開來，但有時並不需要逗號，直接跟在名詞後面即可，President Trump 即為一例，Trump 是 President 的同位語，兩者必須緊緊相連，不能用逗號分開，因為是限定用法。同位語也有非限定用法，特色是要用逗號與它補充說明的名詞或名詞片語分開。

39-1 文法修行 Let's Go

Q39 請問你都怎麼記憶同位語？有什麼更快的學習方式嗎？

「HOW」

■ 同位語中很常見的是跟在某些名詞後面的 that 子句，此時的 that 子句就是一個名詞子句，等同於前面的名詞，功能是用來說明前面的名詞。例如: They got the news that a new English teacher was coming. 但不是每個名詞都可以接作為同位語的 that 子句，常用的有 news, fact, dream, belief, idea: The fact that she did not pass the exam was not acceptable. 作為同位語的 that 子句也可放在主詞的位置，實際上的主詞是 fact，that 子句是在說明什麼樣的事實。

「Extra Bonus」

■ 可以接同位語 that 子句的名詞分為幾類: 表示思考或認識的名詞（belief, concept, feeling, idea, opinion, thought）、表示要求、期望、傳達的名詞（decision, desire, expectation, hope, information, news, report, rumor, suggestion）、其他類（chance, fact, possibility, evidence, proof）。

「HOW」

■ 美國正義兄弟二重唱（The Righteous Brothers）的歌曲〈奔放的旋律〉（Unchained Melody）因作為電影《第六感生死戀》主題曲而傳唱至今，其中唱到: Oh, my love, my darling/I've hungered for your touch/A long, lonely time/Time goes by so slowly（噢，我的愛，我的達令/我渴望妳的碰觸/很長的一段孤寂時間/時間過得這麼慢）

■ 裡面的 my love, my darling 或許可以被視為同位語，但如果改成 you, my love，就毫無疑問地有同位語，即 my love 是 you 的同位語。不然，my love, my darling 只能是呼格詞（vocative）。

「Extra Bonus」

■ 有些人名後面會加一綽號（epithet），這個綽號也是一種同位語。
  · Alexander the Great（亞歷山大大帝，the Great 是 Alexander 的同位語）

「**HOW**」

■ 同位語分為限定和非限定同位語，前者為必要資訊，不需要用逗號或其他標點符號與前行詞分開，如前面提過的例子 President Trump。

■ 非限定同位語通常為補充說明，前後要用逗號或其他標點符號與句子的其他部分分開，例如：Mr. Lin, a college teacher, is the author of a book on psychology. 這裡的位語 a college teacher 前後用逗號與先行詞及 be 動詞分開，是一種補充說明，就算去掉也不會影響句子的文法完整性，也不會讓人看不懂，只不過少了一點資訊，因為同位語補充說明了 Mr. Lin 的職業和身分。

「**Extra Bonus**」

■ 同位語除了用逗號與句子的其他部分分開外，也用冒號：或破折號---。

・ There are two kinds of people: good people and bad people.

39-2 考試一點靈

文 法加油站

■ 用 of 也可表達同位語。把名詞 A 和名詞 B 用 of 連結在一起，像是 the city of New York，此時 A 和 B 是處於對等關係。

· Their idea of establishing new rules is not possible.

■ 名詞並列是一種常見的限定同位語。

· My best friend Peter, a journalist famous for his sharp criticism of the government, does not like to be criticized.（Peter 是 friend 的限定同位語，而 a journalist famous …則是非限定同位語，用來補充說明 Peter）

■ 動名詞也可以作為同位語。

· The best exercise, walking, also costs the least.（walking 是 exercise 的同位語）

實 戰句

❶ The Kata Project,-----collaboration between neuroscientists, animal experts and computer game specialists, offers an immersive experience for post-stroke patients. The heart and soul of the project is a

dolphin named Bandit. Patients control Bandit on a screen, using the game for therapy.

(A) an

(B) a

(C) the

(D) those

中譯

　　卡塔計畫是神經科學家、動物專家、及電腦遊戲專家之間的合作,為中風後的病患提供一種身歷其境的體驗。這個計畫的核心是一個稱為強盜的海豚。病患在電腦螢幕上操控強盜,把這種遊戲當成治療。

考題最前端

　　這題所考的同位語就是前後由逗號與句子其他部分分開來的 a collaboration between…specialists,作為一種非限定的補充説明,它也可以寫成一個形容詞子句: which is a collaboration…specialists。形容詞子句簡化成片語後經常變成同位語,但兩者之間也不盡然一定畫上等號,因為形容詞子句簡化成片語常常成為分詞片語,無法作為同位語。答案是B。

答案:(B)

文 法加油站

■ 不定詞亦能作為同位語。

- His goal in life, to become a millionaire, does not seem to be possible anytime soon.（to become a millionaire 是 goal 的同位語）

■ 有些名詞後面所接的不定詞其實是同位語，這類名詞有 desire, plan, hope 等。

- He has a desire to win the game.

■ 也可以用 or 來表示同位語。

- He likes to read romances, or love stories.

實 戰句

❷ **Parents may be able to see their unborn babies in three dimensional virtual realities for the first time. It is thanks to new technology merging ultra-sound imagery with magnetic resonance imaging (MRI),-----medical imaging technique used to form pictures of the body.**

(A) the

(B) an

(C) a

(D) that

中譯

　　父母或許可以首次用三度空間的虛擬實境影像看到他們尚未出生的寶寶。這是因為有了結合超音波影像和磁共振成像的新科技，那是一種用來構成身體圖像的醫療成像技術。

考題最前端

　　學術文章經常用到非限定的同位語來補充說明某個概念或事物，所以越早熟悉越好。要注意的是冠詞的使用，為什麼答案是不定冠詞 a，而不是定冠詞 the。記住，任何東西第一次提到都是用 a，再次提及才用 the，由於這裡是在介紹一項新科技，大家都還不認識，所以用 a。答案是 C。

答案：(C)

認識名詞子句

單 元概述

何謂名詞子句？有何功能？

名詞子句是一種具有名詞功能的從屬子句，可以作為主詞、直接受詞、間接受詞、介系詞受詞、主詞補語或同位語。名詞子句的引導詞通常有：從屬連接詞（*that, if, whether*）、疑問詞（*when, who, what, why, how, where, which*）、代名詞（*whoever, whomever, whichever, whatever*）。由 *that* 和疑問詞開頭的子句是最常見的名詞子句。

40-1 文法修行 Let's Go

Q3 請問你都怎麼記憶名詞子句？有什麼更快的學習方式嗎？

「HOW」

■ 名詞子句其實不需特別去記憶，因為引導的詞就是那些，數量不算多。但還是不少人一碰到考試就會搞錯，原因就是沒有的搞懂名詞子句。當我們問，Where is your father?這是一個疑問句，Do you know where your farther is?也是一個問句，可是這個問句包含一個疑問詞 where 所引導的名詞子句，作為動詞 know 的受詞。既然是名詞子句，就要用直述句的詞序，而不是疑問句。很多人以為 Do you know where is your father?才是對的，其實是錯的。

「Extra Bonus」

■ 針對上面所說的，如果例句是 We all asked when he got that.我們不能說成 We all asked when did he get that，但在一個情況下可以，也是加了引號: We all asked, "When did he get that?"

「HOW」

■ 澳洲女歌手娜塔莉 · 英博莉亞（Natalie Imbruglia）在她的〈撕裂〉（Torn）這首歌中唱到：Well, you couldn't be that man I adored/You don't seem to know/Seem to care what your heart is for（哎呀，你不是那個我所崇拜的人/你似乎不知道/似乎不在乎你的心在乎是什麼）

■ 歌詞裡的名詞子句 what your heart is for 是動詞 care 的受詞。歌詞裡還有好幾個名詞子句: That's what's going on. 和 This is how I feel. 這兩個名詞子句都是作為主詞補語。

「Extra Bonus」

■ 常常聽到有人說 That's the way it is. 意思是就是這樣了，換個說法，也可以說成: That's how it is. 這裡的 how it is 也是名詞子句。

「HOW」

■ 名詞子句中常見 that 所引導的子句，that 名詞子句部分和之前介紹過的同位語 that 子句有重疊之處。例如: That we did not do well in the singing competition upsets the teacher./The fact that we did not do well in the singing competition upsets the teacher. 這兩個句子意思相同，但在文法上有些差別，前面句子裡的 that 引導的名詞子句是主詞，動詞是 upset，後面句子裡的主詞是 fact，後面的 that 子句是 fact 的同位語，但本質上也是一個名詞子句。有些人會把 fact 省略掉，結果變成和前一個句子一樣。

「Extra Bonus」

■ 有時 that 子句作為主詞的句型可以改為以虛主詞 it 引導的句型。

- That you will become interested in math is likely./It is likely that you will become interested in math.

40-2 考試一點靈

文 法加油站

- 名詞子句最常出現的是 that 引導的子句，可以作為主詞、受詞、及主詞補語。

  · That he behaved courageously in the face of danger won the praise of everyone.

- 作為動詞受詞的 that 子句。

  · The mayor said that he would seek to improve traffic jams.

- 作為兩個受詞中直接受詞的 that 子句。

  · The teacher taught us that haste makes waste.（但不能改成 The teacher taught that haste makes waste to us.）

實 戰句

❶ More than 50 nations, including the U.S., Germany, China, Russia, and India, are developing battlefield robots, or autonomous killing machines. How will these machines tell friend from foe? -----this question goes unanswered by nations developing battlefield robots shows how complicated the situation is.

(A) Whether

(B) If

(C) That

(D) What

中譯

　　美國、德國、中國、俄羅斯、及印度在內的 50 多個國家正在發展戰場機器人或自動殺人武器。這些機器將如何辨識敵我？發展戰場機器人的國家都未能回答此一問題，顯示出情況的複雜性。

考題最前端

　　這段文字有兩個名詞子句，一個是由 that 引導的 That this question goes unanswered by nations developing battlefield robots，另一個是疑問詞 how 引導的 how complicated the situation is，記住 how 名詞子句和疑問句很像，但除了句首是疑問詞加形容詞外，句子的其他部分都和直述句一樣。疑問句是 How complicated is the situation? 名詞子句則是 how complicated the situation is? 所以答案是 C。

答案：(C)

文 法加油站

■ 作為主詞補語的 that 子句。

- My idea is that eating well does not necessarily guarantee health.

■ 功能、用法、及使用頻率類似於 that 子句是 whether 或 if 引導的子句。

- I am not sure whether/if they will come. （也可以寫成 Whether they will come is not certain. 此時 whether 引導的子句作為主詞，但 if 就不能放在句首，所以保險起見，不確定時用 whether 就沒錯。）

■ 作為主詞補語的 whether 引導的子句。

- The question is whether the man is trustworthy.

實 戰句

❷ Views are divided on-----there is a connection between lack of sleep and cancer. Long-term sleep disruptions may raise the risk of some cancers, but sleep and cancer influence each other not necessarily as seriously as we imagine.

(A) that

(B) whether

(C) how

(D) what

中譯

　　缺乏睡眠和癌症間是否有關連，各方意見分歧。長期睡眠不良可能增高某些癌症的風險，但睡眠和癌症的相互影響不見得如我們想像的那般嚴重。

考題最前端

　　這裡考的是 whether 引導的名詞子句。that 子句通常前面不能接介系詞，但 whether 子句就沒有這個限制。that 子句只有少數狀況才會前面接介系詞，譬如: It is important to sleep well in that bad sleep will cause physical or mental disorders.這裡的 in that 是因為的意思。疑問詞引導的名詞子句也可以在前面接介系詞: Views are divided on how lack of sleep and cancer are connected to each other.但改成這樣就和原句的意思不同。答案是 B。

答案：(B)

認識副詞子句

單 元概述

何謂副詞子句？有何功能？

副詞子句是從屬連接詞所引導的從屬子句，功能是在修飾主要子句，所以才稱為副詞子句。連接副詞子句的從屬連接詞有表示條件的 if, as long as, unless、表示時間的 when, before, after, since, until、表示地方的 where、表示目的的 so that, in order that, lest, in case、表示原因的 because, as, so, so... that、表示讓步的 although, though, even though, whether 等。

41-1 文法修行 **Let's Go**

Q41 請問你都怎麼記憶副詞子句？有什麼更快的學習方式嗎？

「**HOW**」

■ 副詞子句作為修飾主要子句的從屬子句，位置可以放在句首或句尾，有時也放在句中，但對文法沒那麼熟悉的人，在寫作時還是不要嘗試把副詞子句放在句中，以免出錯。

■ 不過副詞子句放在句首的機會通常比較多，譬如: Because he came late, we had to cancel the meeting./We had to cancel the meeting because he came late. 放在句首可以強化語氣，比較有力，其次，副詞子句放在句首，要用逗號和後面的主要子句分開，放在句中則不用逗號和前面的主要子句分開。

「**Extra Bonus**」

■ 表示目的的副詞子句通常放在句尾。

- Henry got up early so that he could catch the bus.

■ 美國已故黑人女歌手惠特妮‧休士頓（Whitney Houston）在她經典的歌曲〈時間上那一刻〉（One Moment In Time）中唱到: I want one moment in time/When I'm more than I thought I could be/When all of my dreams are a heartbeat away（我想要時間上那一刻/當我比我自認為擁有的更多的那一刻/當我所有夢想只有一個心跳距離的那一刻）

■ 這裡有關係副詞 when 引導的子句，看起來很像副詞子句，其實是形容詞子句，不要看到 when 就以為是副詞子句。

「Extra Bonus」

■ 關係副詞 when 也可以引導一個從屬子句來修飾前面的先行詞，像是歌詞裡 I want one moment in time when I'm more than I thought I could be.

「**HOW**」

■ 副詞子句中表示時間的子句最常用 as, when, while 來表示當...時,這三個從屬連接詞表面上看起來意思一樣,實際上還有差別。它們引導的副詞子句如果放在句首,要用逗號和後面的主要子句分開,如果放在句尾,就不需要用逗號和前面的主要子句分開。

■ when 通常指時間比較短的動作的狀態,而主要子句則是持續的動作或狀態,例如: He was listening to the music when he heard the explosion. 至於 as 和 while 則表達持續比較長的動作或狀態,例如: I often got up early while I studied in the U.S.

「**Extra Bonus**」

■ 現在越來越有用 as 來表示當…時的趨勢,有時也用來表達原因或附屬的狀態。

· As we grow older, we must eat less meat to stay healthy.

41-2 考試一點靈

文 法加油站

- 表示地方的副詞子句由 where 或 wherever 引導。

  · Where there is smoke, there is fire.

- 表示時間的副詞子句，引導的從屬連接詞除了 when, while, as 外，還有 till, until, since, after, before, as soon as，用法大致相同，但也有不同之處。以 since 為例，通常主要子句要用完成式來表示持續一段時間的動作或狀態。

  · He has been very busy since he got the new job.

- as soon as 給人感覺好像只能放在句尾，其實句首也能擺，所表達的是比主要子句更早的動作，有時意義相當於 after。

  · We always have a cold drink as soon as we get to the beach.

實 戰句

❶ A study carried out by researchers at the University of Montreal indicated that playing "shooter" games can damage the hippocampus area of the brain. Young people might be put at greater risk of dementia-----they grow older.

(A) if

(B) as

(C) so

(D) since

中譯

　　一項由蒙特婁大學研究員所做的研究顯示，玩「射擊」遊戲可能對腦部海馬區造成傷害。年輕人隨著年紀變大罹患痴呆症的風險也就更大。

考題最前端

　　之前提過 as 除了表示當…時，還有隨著或因為的意思，用途非常廣泛，現在普遍用於學術性文章或新聞報導中。雖說 as 和 when 可以相互替換，但這裡不能說成 when they grow older，因為用 when 表示他們要到了比較大的年紀才會有癡呆症的風險，用 as 則是表示隨著年紀漸增，癡呆症的風險也會逐漸增大，這才是研究的結果。答案是 B。

答案：(B)

■ 表示原因的副詞子句由 because, as, since, in case 引導。

- Since you do not have time, we will have to give the case to someone else.

■ 表示結果的副詞子句由 so…that, such…that 引導。

- He worked so hard that he got a pay raise./He is such a hard-working student that he has little time to take exercise.（注意 so 和 such 的用法不同）

■ 表示目的的副詞子句由 so that, in order that 引導。

- Henry studied hard so that he could be admitted to the best university.

實 戰句

❷ **Data from NASA's Lunar Reconnaissance Orbiter helps scientists identify bright areas in craters near the moon's south pole, indicating the possible presence of surface frost. How old the moon's ice is? The water on the moon,-----delivered by icy comets or asteroids, could be as ancient as the solar system.**

(A) since

(B) though

(C) so

(D) if

中譯

美國太空總署月球勘測軌道飛行器所蒐集的數據協助科學家確認月球南極附近隕石坑裡的亮區有可能是表面結霜所致。月球上的冰有多老？月球上的水如果是由結冰的彗星或小行星所帶來，可能和太陽系一樣老。

考題最前端

之前提過副詞子句也可放在句中，但有相當的難度，如果沒有把握就不要輕易嘗試。這裡就有一個現成的例子，if delivered by icy comets or asteroids 是簡化自 if 子句 if it was delivered by icy comets or asteroids。副詞子句簡化成片語的原則就是主詞相同時，去掉副詞子句的主詞，如果動詞是 be 動詞也去掉，一般動詞則改成 Ving。答案是 D。

答案：(D)

了解搭配語

單 元概述

何謂搭配語？有何功能？

搭配語（collocation）有點像是慣用語（idiom）或固定用語（fixed expression），但範圍更大，泛指字詞一般的搭配方式，有時不是文法對錯的問題，而是道不道地的問題，像是紅茶的英文是 black tea，而不是 red tea，這就是一種 collocation。為什麼老菸槍是 heavy smoker，而不是 strong smoker，外國人可能不覺得有太大差別，可是以英語為母語者就無法接受這種不道地的說法。

42-1 文法修行 Let's Go

Q42 請問你都怎麼記憶搭配語？有什麼更快的學習方式嗎？

「**HOW**」

■ 搭配語有好幾種：

❶ 形容詞加名詞（rotten apples, regular exercise）

❷ 名詞加動詞（Snow falls./ Wind blows）

❸ 動詞加名詞（do homework, take a shower）

❹ 副詞加形容詞（fully aware, completely satisfied）

❺ 名詞加名詞（television license, milk chocolate）

❻ 動詞加副詞或副詞加動詞（rain heavily, whisper softly）。

■ 其中又以動詞加名詞的 collocation 最常出現，如 do an exercise, do a favor, do a business, do one's best, make arrangements, make an attempt, make a choice, make a comment，換句話說可以用 do 和 make 這些常用的動詞組合成許多的搭配語，就這一點而言有點像是片語動詞。

「**Extra Bonus**」

■ 片語動詞是動詞加介系詞組成的多字動詞，搭配語是慣常的說法，不只有動詞。

■ commit a crime 和 make a mistake 是搭配語，不是片語動詞。

「HOW」

■ 英國的老牌警察樂團（The Police）在他們經典的歌曲〈你的每次呼吸〉（Every Breath You Take）中唱到:Every breath you take/Every move you make/Every bond you break/Every step you take/I'll be watching you（你的每次呼吸/妳做的每個動作/妳斷的每個關係/妳走的每一步/我都將看著妳）

■ 裡面的詞語幾乎都是來自一些搭配語，像是 take a breath 衍生為 every breath you take，make a move 衍生為 every move you make，break a bond 衍生為 every bond you break，take a step 衍生為 every step you take。這首歌幾乎可以當成一首學習英文搭配詞的最佳歌曲。

「Extra Bonus」

■ 歌詞裡還有其他搭配語，如 every single day, every word you day（演變自 say a word）、every game you play（演變自 play a game）。相當奇妙的一首歌，應有盡有。

「HOW」

■ 搭配語不同於片語動詞已經在前面說過，至於和固定用語及慣用語之間的差別，則是搭配語的組成及用法比較靈活和廣泛，固定用語及慣用語比較死。

■ 舉例來說，pleased to meet you, all of a sudden, on the other hand 等都是固定用語，是某些情況下的標準說法。pull someone's leg, a can of worms 等則是慣用語，它們的意思經常從字面上看不出來，也從組成的個別字無法看出意義，但搭配語則是淺顯易懂，是日常慣用的說法，通常不會有太深的引申意義。

「Extra Bonus」

■ 以 work 為例，work in progress, work like a dog 是慣用語，labor-intensive work, dirty work, work ethic 則是搭配語。

・ She has a really good work ethic. She works like a dog.

42-2 考試一點靈

文 法加油站

■ 搭配語的最基本形式就是一些慣用的說法，如 heavy rain（不是 think rain）、high temperature（不是 tall temperature）、scenic view（不是 scenic picture）。

- She was discharged from hospital.（不是 She was released from hospital）

■ 一些常用的動詞，如 make, do, take，可以組成許多的搭配語，像是 do homework, make change, take a shower。

- I like to take showers in the mornings and baths in the evenings.（搭配語可以有變化，像是把 take a shower 改成 take showers，慣用語和固定用語就沒有這種彈性）

■ 搭配語可以拆開來重新排列組合，慣用語和固定用語則不行，像是 every breath you take（變化自 take a breath）。

- The kind of job he undertakes is labor-intensive work.（也可以說成 His job is labor-intensive.）

實 戰句

❶ **We all know exercise is good for health. Even a little exercise-----a difference. U.S. and global guidelines call for 150 minutes of moderate or 75 minutes of vigorous exercise each week. Even less frequent exercise can help reduce risk of death from heart disease and other causes.**

(A) does
(B) takes
(C) makes
(D) do

中譯

　　我們都知道運動有益於健康，即使一點點運動也會造成差別。美國和全球的指導原則要求每周 150 分鐘的中度或 75 分鐘的劇烈運動。即使運動量沒那麼頻繁還是能幫助降低死於心臟病及其他疾病的機率。

考題最前端

　　可以於 make a difference 中間插入形容詞修飾 difference，例如：Higher wages would make a big difference to our living standards. 也可以使用 huge 等形容詞。也可以構成問句，譬如: What difference does it make?答案是 C。

答案：(C)

文 法加油站

■ 形容詞加名詞也可以組成許多的搭配語，如 heavy traffic/rain/snow、
 a strong person/animal/wind/current、a rich man/history/culture。

 ・This place has a rich history and culture.

■ 再來複習一下，搭配語就是最合乎英文習慣的字詞組合，有些我們在
 台灣學的可能不是真正的英文用法。

 例如：要説 the fast train, fast food，而不是 the quick train, quick
 food; 要説 a quick shower, a quick meal，而不是 a fast shower, a
 fast meal。

■ 一些常用的動詞搭配語看起來有點像片語動詞或動詞片語，其實不
 是。它們有 feel free, save time, make progress, do the washing up。

 ・Please feel free to take a seat and enjoy the view.

實 戰句

❷ With every drop of water we drink and every breath we take, we are connected to the sea. Rising sea levels due to global warming could take a-----on coastal areas and cause substantial economic losses.

(A) tall

(B) toll

(C) tale

(D) tide

中譯

　　我們所喝的每一滴水及所吸的每口空氣，都和海洋有關。全球暖化所造成的海平面上升將對沿岸地區造成傷害，引發重大的經濟損失。

考題最前端

　　短文裡的 take a toll 也是動詞加名詞的搭配語，後面接介系詞 on，表示對後面的事物造成傷害。同樣地，take a toll 中間也能加形容詞來加以修飾，像是 take a terrible toll 或 take a heavy toll。當我們說 Certain diseases take a heavy toll on life.意思是某些疾病會造成重大的生命損失。答案是 B。

答案：(B)

國家圖書館出版品預行編目(CIP)資料

新托福100⁺ iBT文法 / 許貴運著. -- 初版.
-- 臺北市：倍斯特, 2017.11　面；　公分. --
（考用英語系列；4）
ISBN 978-986-95288-5-6（平裝）

1.托福考試　2.語法

805.1894　　　　　　　　　　106017924

考用英語系列　004

新托福100　iBT文法

初　　版	2017年11月
定　　價	新台幣399元

作　　者	許貴運
出　　版	倍斯特出版事業有限公司
發 行 人	周瑞德
電　　話	886-2-2351-2007
傳　　真	886-2-2351-0887
地　　址	100 台北市中正區福州街1號10樓之2
E - m a i l	best.books.service@gmail.com
官　　網	www.bestbookstw.com
執行總監	齊心瑀
行銷經理	楊景輝
企劃編輯	陳韋佑
封面構成	高鍾琪
內頁構成	菩薩蠻數位文化有限公司
印　　製	大亞彩色印刷製版股份有限公司

港澳地區總經銷	泛華發行代理有限公司
地　　址	香港新界將軍澳工業邨駿昌街7號2樓
電　　話	852-2798-2323
傳　　真	852-2796-5471